CW00349389

Werewolves Were Only in Stories

But in a way, Jenna was sorry they didn't exist—imagine the challenge of trying to tame one.

You'd probably have to start with a young werewolf, she thought. Easier to train. Of course it certainly would be inconvenient if the creature turned human when he was pulling a sled!

And if he were an adult male werewolf—she could almost picture him, silvery gray, with slanted yellow-green eyes—what would he look like when he changed into a man...?

A dark figure walked into the moonlight.

"Who are you?" Jenna demanded with a slight quaver.

"Weylin Matthews," he said, his gaze intent.

How bright green his eyes were, Jenna noted, almost incandescent. Their gleam shut everything else from her consciousness. *If the werewolf sees you first, you'll be struck dumb....*

Dear Reader:

SILHOUETTE DESIRE is an exciting new line of contemporary romances from Silhouette Books. During the past year, many Silhouette readers have written in telling us what other types of stories they'd like to read from Silhouette, and we've kept these comments and suggestions in mind in developing SILHOUETTE DESIRE.

DESIREs feature all of the elements you like to see in a romance, plus a more sensual, provocative story. So if you want to experience all the excitement, passion and joy of falling in love, then SILHOUETTE DESIRE is for you.

For more details write to:

Jane Nicholls
Silhouette Books
PO Box 236
Thornton Road
Croydon
Surrey CR9 3RU

DIANA STUART
Leader of the Pack

Silhouette Desire

Originally Published by Silhouette Books
division of
Harlequin Enterprises Ltd.

*All the characters in this book have no existence outside the
imagination of the Author, and have no relation whatsoever to
anyone bearing the same name or names. They are not even dis-
tantly inspired by any individual known or unknown to the Author,
and all the incidents are pure invention.*

*The text of this publication or any part thereof may not be repro-
duced or transmitted in any form or by any means, electronic or
mechanical, including photocopying, recording, storage in an
information retrieval system, or otherwise, without the written
permission of the publisher.*

*This book is sold subject to the condition that it shall not, by way
of trade or otherwise, be lent, resold, hired out or otherwise cir-
culated without the prior consent of the publisher in any form of
binding or cover other than that in which it is published and
without a similar condition including this condition being imposed
on the subsequent purchaser.*

DIANA STUART
lives in the Hudson River Highlands and has been publishing gothic and adventure novels since 1973. A nurse, she's fascinated by Indian culture. She is a native Californian.

Another Silhouette Book by Diana Stuart

Silhouette Desire

A Prime Specimen

For further information about
Silhouette Books please write to:

Jane Nicholls
Silhouette Books
PO Box 236
Thornton Road
Croydon
Surrey CR9 3RU

Dear Reader:
While I was writing this book, an Alaskan woman, Libby Riddles, won the Iditarod, making her the first woman to win the 1,135 mile dog sled race. Cheers, Libby!

One

The full moon's light silvered the snow, transforming the spruce-covered slopes of the Chugach Mountains into a moonlit fantasy land. Twenty miles of snowy wilderness lay between Jenna Henderson's camp and Anchorage, and she savored the clear, chill solitude—or would be savoring it if her blasted lead dog ever stopped acting up.

"You behave, Chingo," she warned. "Now!"

Sullenly the rangy black husky, alpha male of the pack, submitted to her tugging and allowed her to chain him to the line where the other sled dogs were resting in the snow. Jenna stepped back and checked the picket chain, stretched between two trees, then surveyed the dogs. None seemed particularly tired. All had performed excellently that day.

Except Chingo.

Jenna hadn't been tired either until she'd had to haul and tug at Chingo to get him chained. Dragging a stubborn sixty-pound husky around wasn't her idea of what a trainer should be doing at the end of a run. She'd never had so much trouble with a dog before.

"If you weren't such a good leader I swear I'd drop you back to wheel position and give Sonia your job," she muttered.

The dog's slanting dark eyes challenged her. Jenna sighed and headed for the sack of dog food still on the sled. It wasn't too cold by Alaskan standards; the tiny thermometer dangling from the zipper of her parka pocket hovered around ten above zero. Of course, it was only late November. The Chippewa Indians in her former home state of Minnesota would call this Lake-Freezing Moon. Come to think of it, except for its runners, her sled wasn't so very different from the old Chippewa *nobugidaban*, "toboggan," also dog-powered.

In front of her tent a small fire snapped, the yellow flames cheery in the chill night. Overhead the aurora borealis blazed a narrow trail of cold blue light across the sky. Pathway of the Spirits, to the Chippewa. Jenna wondered what Alaskan Indians and Eskimos called the northern lights. She knew a little about the Eskimos but almost nothing about the Indians. Maybe after the big race she'd have time to take a class in native culture at the University of Alaska.

When she'd finished feeding and watering the dogs, Jenna cooked her own meal. She'd decided to try champion musher George Attla's trail dinner—a small steak, cut-up potatoes, and a chunk of butter all wrapped in aluminum foil and tossed into a blazing fire. Cook fifteen minutes, he'd said. She allowed a few extra.

The steak and potatoes turned out to be a tasty change from dehydrated trail food. Jenna finished with hot tea and felt invigorated. Though the dogs were curled up on the spruce boughs she'd cut for them, she wasn't ready to crawl into her down sleeping bag inside the tent.

The Chugach Mountains rose around her, their barren peaks whitened by snow. The dogs were quiet; there was no sound except for the pop of the fire. Jenna took a deep breath and watched the white plume float upward as she exhaled. She huddled deeper into her scarlet parka.

"Red Riding Hood," some of the other mushers had taken to calling her. She glanced at the darkness of the spruce woods surrounding her and smiled. Red Riding Hood was in her proper habitat.

Somewhere in the distance a wolf howled; she started momentarily at the sound, then chuckled. So was the wolf. Jenna listened for the lupine chorus that should follow but heard nothing. A solo wolf was a rarity; the animals almost always traveled in packs. The wolf called again, a long quavering howl that echoed in her head long after the sound faded into the silence of the Alaskan night.

Into her mind crept the memory of stories told beside Girl Scout campfires when she was young, with the Minnesota woods rising darkly all around.

One tale had been about a werewolf who stalked lone campers on nights of the full moon, howling like a wolf while walking upright like a man.

I'm the perfect werewolf victim, she told herself wryly. A woman camping alone in the Chugaches, miles from anywhere. The moon is full, I've heard the beast's eerie cry. . . .

She shook her head. Werewolves were only stories, and real wolves didn't attack humans. In a way she was sorry werewolves didn't exist—imagine the challenge and excitement of trying to tame one.

You'd probably have to start with a young werewolf, just as puppies were easier to train than adult dogs. Of course there might be a problem when the creature turned human again. It certainly would be inconvenient if you had the beast pulling a sled at the time.

And, if he was an adult male werewolf—she could almost picture him, silvery gray with slanted yellow-green eyes, a magnificent animal—what would he look like when he changed into a man?

Dog chains rattled. Chingo leaped to his feet and began a frenzied barking. Seconds later all fourteen dogs joined in. Jenna turned away from the fire, staring into the blackness between the spruces surrounding her. What had set the dogs off?

A dark figure walked from the cover of the trees into the moonlight and stood poised no more than ten feet from her. Jenna froze, the feel of icy hands on her back. What was it she saw? Werewolves didn't exist; only bears and men walked on two legs, and this was no bear.

A man. But why were the dogs going wild over scenting a man? And where could he have come from? She was a good twenty miles from Anchorage, nowhere near a road or a cabin, and she hadn't heard the whine of a snow machine. Lines she'd read somewhere sprang into her head:

"...he howled fearfully
Said he was a wolf, only the difference
Was, a wolf's skin was hairy on the outside,
His on the inside..."

He advanced toward her, moving with the telltale glide of a man on snowshoes. Ignoring the snarling dogs, he passed them and came into the light of the fire. She stared into green eyes set slightly aslant under heavy black brows.

Jenna swallowed, pulling herself together. "Who are you?" she demanded, fighting to control the quaver in her voice.

"Weylin Matthews." He kicked off the snowshoes and straightened up, his eyes intent on hers. Silence thickened the air between them, the white cloud of his breath mingling with hers.

How bright a green his eyes were, almost incandescent, glowing. Their gleam shut everything else from her consciousness.

If the werewolf sees you first, you'll be struck dumb. Another esoteric fragment of werewolfery had popped into her head. Couldn't she think of anything else? With an effort, Jenna forced words past her dry throat. "How did you get here?"

"My snow machine broke down. I followed your trail."

Reverberations from his low voice seemed to settle in her chest, making her heart flutter. His name sounded vaguely familiar. Wait, didn't Weylin mean son of the wolf in some language or other? She knew she'd never met him; she wouldn't have forgotten that lean, handsome face, framed now by his fur-trimmed parka. Wolf fur, by the look of it.

Whoever he was, she was alone with him, a stranger, in an isolated night camp. Jenna edged warily toward her tent where she'd left the knife she always carried on the trail.

"You've put me to a lot of trouble, Jenna Henderson," he growled, stopping her in her tracks.

She blinked at him. How did he know her name? What was he talking about?

His brows drew together, nearly meeting above a chiseled nose. "Why did you take the dogs out when you knew I was coming?" The words snapped out like the crack of a whip.

She shook her head. "I don't know what you're talking about."

"I flew from Whittaker headquarters in L.A. to this godforsaken country solely to check out Maki Equipment. Surely you're aware that Whittaker Enterprises has just taken over your company in Anchorage."

"It's not my company. I did hear Maki Equipment was being sold, but what's that got to do with me taking Mr. Maki's dogs on a training run?"

Weylin Matthews—she now recalled Mr. Maki mentioning that name—started to speak, then hesitated. He tucked his gloved hands underneath his armpits while he looked up and down. Snow slid from a spruce branch, hitting the ground with a soft whoosh, and he whirled to glance at the trees before confronting her again.

"What the hell are you doing camping out in this weather?" he demanded.

"The dogs need conditioning for the Iditarod."

"What's that supposed to mean?"

"The Iditarod race is in early March."

Weylin's green eyes narrowed. "You're training the dogs to race?"

"More for endurance than for speed. The Iditarod is over a thousand-mile run."

"A thousand miles on a dog sled in this country in March." He gazed deliberately at the snow-laden spruces surrounding the fire and beyond at the Chugach peaks. "A man would have to be crazy to make that run."

Jenna bristled. "Do I look crazy?"

"*You're* planning to take the dogs on a trip like that? I don't believe it."

"I have every intention of running the Iditarod." Her tone was as cold as the night wind. "And I won't be the first woman to do so. I'll have you know I'm well qualified. I've won dog sled races in Kalkaska, Michigan, and in Ely, Minnesota. Last year I took a fourth at the Rondy here in Anchorage—that's the big midwinter Fur Rendezvous; the city goes all out to celebrate. Anyway, Mr. Maki wouldn't have offered me the job if he didn't think I—"

"Those other races—are they as long as this Iditarod?"

Jenna took a deep breath, forcing down her anger. Weylin Matthews was the greenest of *cheechakos*. He'd rushed after her at night in a faulty snow machine without considering what he'd do if he had problems. A mad impulse and, in this country, a potentially fatal one. He didn't know the first thing about Alaska, much less about dog sled racing. She must try to be patient, even if his insinuation that a woman couldn't run a team in the Iditarod had riled her.

"Mr. Matthews, I've spent most of my life with dogs, and a good part of it training them. I'm accustomed to cold climates and I'm trailwise. I realize this might be hard for a non-dog person to understand, but to be able to be in the race from Anchorage to Nome is the dream of all mushers."

"And you're planning to race with Maki's dogs."

It wasn't a question but she nodded. "That's why I took the job, to have the chance, even if the dogs aren't mine. What I still don't understand is why you felt you had to track me down."

He didn't answer, turning away from her to look toward the picket line where most of the huskies had settled down again except for Chingo and his mate, the fawn-and-white female named Sonia. They were still on their feet, eyes fixed on Weylin.

"You really startled the dogs when you came into camp," Jenna said, not mentioning her own upset.

"They probably smelled the wolf scent."

Her mouth dropped open.

Don't be an idiot, she admonished herself. He means the wolf you heard howling—he must have heard it too.

"I don't know what went wrong with the snow machine," Weylin said. "Usually I can get anything mechanical started again, but it's just too damned cold here." Weylin held out his hands to the fire. "You freeze to death if you take a glove off. I guess you're stuck with me for the night." He smiled, white teeth in a California-tan face. The better to eat you with, my dear?

Nonsense. But he was right about having to remain at her camp. In her surprise and confusion over his arrival, she hadn't thought about that problem. She

had a one-woman tent and a one-woman sleeping bag.
The tent alone wasn't enough protection in ten-degree
weather, not for sleeping, although the bag was. Even
if she'd wanted to share the sleeping bag with him—
and she assuredly did not—its small size made that
impossible.

She eyed him. He was taller than she by a couple of
inches, so he probably was about five ten. The down-
filled parka made it hard to tell, but he looked lean.
The fur-trimmed hood hid his hair, and she found
herself wondering what color it was. Black like his
eyebrows, or silver gray?

Come on, she warned herself. Stop that. He may be
a *cheechako*, but he's no werewolf.

"You might fit into my sleeping bag," she told him.
"I had it custom made for me, but if you scrunched up
some you might make it."

"The two of us, you mean?"

Her face flamed. "No!" The thought of being inside the bag with this disturbing man made her pulses
pound.

"It's a one-person sleeping bag," she said, doing
her best to be brisk.

"Then I wouldn't dream of denying you its use."
His tone mocked her, and the slight smile on his face
was infuriating.

"You're not dressed for a night that might go down
to zero," she pointed out. "You really shouldn't have
taken the snow machine onto the trail without warmer
boots and pants. And mitts instead of gloves."

"I didn't expect trouble."

"In this country you have to be prepared for trouble or else you won't survive. I suppose you wouldn't
understand that, coming as you do from California."

"Are you giving me an excuse or making a snide remark?"

"To be honest, both."

His green eyes danced with amusement. Behind the amusement she glimpsed quite a different emotion. Was it desire? Her breath caught.

"How long have you been in Alaska, Jenna?"

"Two years. Long enough so I'm no longer a *cheechako*, a greenhorn."

"Meaning I am?"

She nodded. "All newcomers are. You can't learn about the country overnight—it's not like moving from Minnesota to Wisconsin or from California to Arizona."

"Maybe you can teach me how to survive in Alaska."

"I wasn't aware you'd be here that long."

"It depends. I can see where it might take me longer than I thought." His eyes flicked over her white quilted ski overalls and red parka and came to rest on her face. She had the impression he was trying to imagine what lay under her winter garb.

"To evaluate Maki Equipment?" she asked deliberately.

He gave her a one-sided smile. "What else?"

"You still haven't explained why you drove after me. What do the dogs have to do with the Whittaker take-over?"

His smile faded. "The dogs—" He broke off, shaking his head. "I just couldn't imagine anyone taking dogs out to spend the night in the snow miles from town. I wanted to see for myself."

The explanation didn't satisfy her. A sense of unease settled over Jenna. Why *was* he there?

"What got you started in dog racing anyway?" he asked, shifting position to ram his hands into his pockets.

"I told you, I've always had dogs around—my uncle back in Ely is a veterinarian. When I was fourteen, he let my brother and me try to teach a litter of Samoyed puppies to pull a sled. We made a lot of mistakes and learned as much from the pups as they did from us, but I'll never forget the thrill of standing on the sled runners and having those half-grown Samoyeds actually pull me. I became a musher right then and there."

"A musher being a dog sled racer?"

She nodded. "If you try it once, you'll never be the same."

"Maybe so." His tone told her he doubted she was right. "I'm not up here to play games with dogs but to take a good long look at Maki Equipment. If I survive long enough in this cold."

"I can make you hot tea."

He shook his head impatiently. "Maki Equipment's no different than any other company Whittaker's taken over, and we've a standard policy of paring the excess trappings of new acquisitions. Stripping off the frills. Companies are in business to make money, not to indulge their owners' fancies."

Jenna shrugged. She supposed he had a point. "So you're the hatchet man who chops away at all the little companies Whittaker acquires?"

He frowned. "I hadn't thought of it in exactly that way."

"Do you enjoy it?"

"It's not a matter of enjoyment. The method works for Whittaker, that's all."

"Yet here you are freezing in a night camp on the side of a mountain without gear and surrounded by dogs. Why didn't you stay in Anchorage chopping away?"

"The dogs should have been in the kennels where Maki thought they were. He told me you had them out, but he couldn't tell me when you'd be back with them. 'Maybe tomorrow or the next day,' he said. What kind of schedule is that?"

"Mr. Maki has never required me to report to him each time I take the dogs on the trail. He prefers not to be bothered with details."

"No way to run a company," her uninvited guest muttered, stomping his boots on the snow. "My left foot's gone numb."

Jenna fought down her annoyance. It really was none of Weylin Matthews's business what she did with the dogs, but there was little point in arguing when it was obvious he was slowly freezing. Serve him right for dashing after her when he could have been comfortable in a warm hotel room, probably a suite at the Captain Cook. Instead, she was stuck with him for the night.

Since he wouldn't try the sleeping bag, she could think of only one way to keep them both fairly warm. She would have to strike the tent, lay it over spruce boughs, and wrap it around the two of them, with the insulation pad and sleeping bag on top. She'd build up the fire and they'd lie with their feet toward it.

The trouble was, she wasn't eager to spend the night snuggled against Weylin. Something about him affected her all too potently. Never mind how many layers of clothing would separate her from him; they'd still be too close together to suit her.

"If we took down the tent," Weylin put in, "couldn't we—"

"I'm planning to do that." Her voice was sharp. She didn't need a *cheechako*'s advice. His uninvited presence in her camp was enough of a problem.

What was there about this green-eyed man that fascinated her against her will? Dog sledding was still largely a man's sport, so she'd had her share of overt and covert propositions from fellow racers, but she'd learned as a girl in Minnesota growing up among men how to deflect a male before he got started.

Never before, though, had any man aroused such strong and conflicting emotions in her as Weylin did. An alpha male, that's what he was, needing to dominate. She glanced at Chingo, who'd finally curled up to sleep, nose tucked into his bushy tail.

A stubborn alpha male.

At the same time she couldn't deny the attraction that flared between her and Weylin, as pulsing and highly charged as the northern lights overhead. Gazing at him, she felt threatened by the flames reflected in his eyes. Weylin forced himself to look away from Jenna Henderson's large brown eyes. A man could lose himself in their dark depths. In the bulky winter clothes she wore, he couldn't see much of her except those eyes, but they'd been enough to throw him off course.

It was obvious she didn't know the truth about the dogs. Why hadn't he come right out and told her? He'd certainly intended to; he'd chosen a number of choice phrases as he struggled to master the art of snowshoeing after the damn snow machine cut out on him. Where had all his irritation gone, his annoyance at this dog trainer who'd defied him by not having the animals on hand for him to inspect when he'd arrived in Anchorage?

Not merely annoyance either—it was anger that had driven him onto the trail after her, a determination to track her down, not to wait idly in Anchorage for her to appear at her convenience. Damn it, he was in charge; she wasn't.

He stared into the night sky, watching the shifting brilliance of the aurora borealis as it arced across the heavens. Anchorage had been just another city, but this outlying mountainous wilderness was alien to him. Beautiful in its way, but cold as hell. No wonder the snow machine had malfunctioned; he felt disoriented himself.

Not from the cold, Matthews. Admit it, it's the woman, not the weather.

It wasn't his style to equivocate. He should have told her right away. If he had though, the sparkle of enthusiasm in those lovely brown eyes would have blinked out—she was really involved in this dog sled racing. Besides, she'd have blamed him instead of the real culprit—Maki—and he'd have lost any chance of seeing her again once they got back to Anchorage. If they ever did. Damn, it was cold.

He wanted to see her again, wanted to know how she looked without her arctic garb. Maki had told him a little about her: twenty-three, B.S. in biology from the University of Minnesota—she'd gone through in three years. A photograph of her with the dogs on Maki's desk had shown a serious young woman with her blond hair in coronet braids. The picture gave no hint of the way her brown eyes could flash with anger or how they'd widened with startled awareness when she gazed into his. He sure as hell wasn't going back to California without investigating just what it was that had passed between them at that moment.

At the same time, he had no intention of changing his mind about the dogs. Policy was policy. Seeing Jenna striking the tent, Weylin hurried to help her spread it over a pile of boughs, the aromatic scent of spruce rising to his nostrils.

"We'll lie here," she said, "with our feet to the fire, and we'll wrap the sides of the tent around us, plus the sleeping bag."

Was there a hint of a tremor in that matter-of-fact voice? He tried to read her expression, but she avoided looking directly at him. He smiled slightly at the realization that she was upset about lying next to him. She wasn't as much in command as she pretended.

"I really don't see anything amusing in the situation," Jenna snapped.

His smile faded, not so much because of her words as from the sudden knowledge of how much he wanted to lie close to her, to put his arms around her, down parka and all. In his thirty-one years he didn't recall being so attracted to a woman on such short acquaintance. And all without being able to see much of her except her fur-framed face, which was certainly worth more than a glance. Jenna's high forehead, her huge dark eyes, short straight nose, and softly rounded lips added up to a very appealing face.

Minutes later, after he'd helped her pull the collapsed tent and the sleeping bag over them as they lay side by side, Weylin found himself totally unamused. There was nothing funny about being encased in layers of clothes you couldn't remove for fear of freezing to death and then to discover how intensely you wanted the woman next to you, who was also wrapped in a cocoon of clothes.

Clearly a no-win situation.

Jenna tried to relax, but her acute awareness of Weylin's nearness kept her muscles stiff. She cleared her throat.

"Are your feet any warmer?" she asked.

"Everything's warmer." He didn't sound especially pleased.

From the corners of her eyes she could see that his face was turned toward her. She swallowed. He was so close. If she faced him, his lips would be only an inch or two from hers, their breaths would mingle. The pulse in her throat speeded up.

She shifted, turning so she was on her side and facing away from him. She tensed when she felt him move and fit himself to her, spoon fashion. His arm came around her waist to draw her closer to him. She resisted the impulse to push him away. It was really a practical position for keeping warm and, considering all the clothes between them, not exactly intimate. Except that having his body fitted to hers, her back to his front, his arm holding her, made her tingle with anticipation, as though the touch of his gloved hand was the first step of an exciting journey, one she longed to make.

With Weylin Matthews.

No, she chided herself. Stop thinking about him. This is temporary, an emergency measure to keep the two of you warm. It means nothing. Not to you, not to him. Nothing. Turn your attention to more important things, like the Iditarod.

The big race. When she'd been on the trail earlier, she'd pretended she and dogs were running the final lap from Anchorage to Nome, that they'd conquered the mountains and the frigid interior and had reached the Bering Sea. She almost believed she could see the lights of Nome in the distance.

Until Chingo had taken it into his head to challenge her authority by slowing his pace to a walk, oblivious to her order to "hike." She'd had nothing but trouble with him from then on until she'd stopped to camp. She didn't train dogs by beating them, and she'd punished Chingo only by speaking crossly to him, telling him he was a bad dog.

It hadn't worked. Tomorrow she'd have to try another tack.

Tomorrow. Somehow she had to get through the night. Every cell in her body was attuned to the man who cuddled her against him. She was never going to be able to sleep.

What was the story about the strange allure werewolves, whether male or female, possessed when in human form? Something about a woman named White Fell, of such surpassing beauty that no man could resist her and could only follow her to their doom—which came when she changed into a white wolf and savaged them.

Not, Jenna told herself, that she believed Weylin was anything of the sort. Werewolves were the stuff of tales told around campfires; they had no reality.

All the same, she thought, still tensely aware of Weylin's body pressed to hers, there certainly must be such a thing as a strange allure, because she was rapidly becoming a victim of Weylin's.

Two

The Crow's Nest was crowded. Jenna, who'd never been to the restaurant before, turned her gaze from the other diners to look at the view of the city from the long windows beside her table. What else but a window table for Weylin Matthews, she asked herself.

Her lips curved into a smile as she gazed down at the greater part of Anchorage all lit up below her—a true city of lights in winter, when the sun didn't rise before 10:00 A.M. and disappeared about three in the afternoon.

On a summer evening, the view would probably be even more splendid. To the west, across the Knik Arm of Cook Inlet, you'd be able to see Mount Susitna, the Sleeping Lady of the Indians, and to the north if the weather was right, Mount McKinley in all its glory.

The Crow's Nest was on the twentieth floor of the tallest of the three towers of the Captain Cook Hotel.

The hotel to stay in, somehow more Alaskan than the Hilton, and not just because of the ten-foot-tall stuffed Siberian polar bear in the lobby. After all, Captain Cook, searching for the Northwest Passage in 1778, had sailed up the inlet as far as the forested bowl where Anchorage now stood before deciding he hadn't found what he sought.

Naturally, Weylin had a suite in the hotel; he took the best for granted, expected it as his due. Not that she'd seen his suite—no, thank you. Her smile turned wry. Not that he'd asked her there either.

She wasn't exactly certain why she'd accepted his invitation to dinner. She hadn't meant to see him ever again, especially after the way she'd acted three nights before in the Chugaches, breaking camp at one in the morning, hitching the dogs, and hitting the trail for Anchorage in the moonlight, all because of her own fears.

"A penny," Weylin's husky voice said from across the table. "Or are thoughts worth a gold nugget here?"

"Certainly not mine." No way was she going to admit how he'd affected her in that camp. Still affected her, even with the width of the table between them. When his eyes caught hers she was as helpless as an animal in a trapper's snare. And just about as scared. What was happening to her?

Weylin was lithe and lean in his silver-gray jacket and charcoal pants, the olive shirt and tie darkening the green of his eyes. He didn't look Alaskan, but he certainly looked attractive, and from the sidelong glances of some of the women seated near them, it was obvious she wasn't the only one who thought so.

"Is there some unwritten code that says a man has to let his beard grow when he crosses into this state?" Weylin asked.

He was the only clean-shaven man in the restaurant. Jenna smiled at him, admiring the strong lines of his face, the determined thrust of his jaw. She glanced at his hair, lighter than his black eyebrows and streaked with premature gray.

"You'd probably grow a fascinating beard," she mused aloud.

His long, tanned fingers briefly touched his chin before he shook his head. "Not for me." You are though, his gaze suggested.

Jenna looked down at his ringless left hand resting on the red tablecloth. Her eyes widened. Was his index finger really as long as his middle finger? A werewolf trait, like the brows meeting over the nose. Mesmerized, she watched as the hand moved toward her own, stopping just short of touching her. Only then did she realize she'd been holding her breath.

What's the matter with me, she chided herself. What kind of crazy fantasies is he provoking? What's happened to the practical Jenna?

"You really seem to like this cold country," Weylin said. "Ever been to California? It might change your mind."

She shook her head. "I want to live here forever."

She toyed with the stem of her wineglass, fighting two contradictory impulses. She wanted to pour out her love for Alaska, to show him why no other state in the Union could compare, and at the same time she felt it was necessary to keep her inner self concealed from him.

She wondered briefly if that was why every Minnesota Chippewa had more than one name, a name for most people to call him or her by and a secret one, revealed to very few. If a stranger didn't know your real name, he could never control you.

But she wasn't a Chippewa, and neither Weylin nor any other man would ever control her.

Jenna watched Weylin turn his head and stare at the lighted city below. "I'll admit there's a challenge for survival here that's stimulating," he said. "I wondered a few times if I was up to it when you mushed us back to the city in the middle of the night."

"I offered to let you ride in the sled."

"That's the easy way."

"And you never take the easy way?" Even as she asked she knew the answer. Not Weylin.

"That's cheating." He smiled as he spoke, but she wasn't fooled. He meant exactly what he said.

"Maybe you can understand why I want to run the Iditarod, then." Intent on conveying what she felt, Jenna leaned toward him. "Do you know what the race represents?"

"No."

"Well, the trail itself was named after the mining camp of Iditarod. In 1908 they struck gold and two years later had a settlement of 2,500 people. Trails wound between Seward, Knik, Iditarod, and Nome, connecting the surrounding gold fields. Dog sleds carried the mail between the settlements and also packed gold to be shipped out of Seward."

"I'd think they'd have used planes once they were available."

"Oh, they did. But a plane can't fly in a snowstorm, whereas a dog sled can mush through. That's what happened in 1925 when Nome had a diphtheria epidemic and blizzards kept planes on the ground. The mail drivers and their dogs carried diphtheria serum from Anchorage to Nome during one of the worst blizzards of that decade. The Iditarod race today celebrates their heroic run.''

''I remember reading about that as a kid! I can't remember the man's name, but his lead dog was called Balto.'' Weylin grinned. ''I haven't thought about that story in years. Funny, the dog made more of an impression on me than the man did.''

''His name was Leonhard Seppala but neither he nor the native mushers who all relayed the serum could have made it without the dogs. Balto deserves to have his statue in New York's Central Park. I went to see it once, and the wonderful thing about it is that it's a statue of just a dog.'' She looked at Weylin, who raised his eyebrows.

''You're implying a dog is not only man's best friend but actually his superior?''

Jenna scowled. Was he mocking her enthusiasm? Didn't Weylin like dogs? She'd have little in common with such a man.

The man she'd always pictured as her ideal would be one who'd feel toward dogs as she did, a sense of love and empathy. Not that she'd been considering Weylin as a possibility for that ideal role. He definitely wasn't in the running. In fact, she wasn't sure she even liked him.

Let's get the evening over with, she advised herself, straightening and picking up the menu. She blinked momentarily when she saw that it was in French, then realized she could translate enough of it to order without help.

"I have the feeling I flunked a test," Weylin said.

"Crab d'Alaska Veronique sounds wonderful," Jenna told him, ignoring his remark. "Don't you think so?"

"If you like grapes with seafood."

Was that a criticism of her taste? Or was he implying she didn't know what she was ordering? Jenna's chin rose. With an effort she held back a tart rejoinder. The sooner the meal was over the better. Whatever had made her think she'd enjoy an evening with Weylin Matthews?

Once Weylin had ordered for them he studied Jenna's oval face. She was clearly annoyed with him; the hint of a frown marred her forehead and turned down the corners of her delightfully full lips. He'd made the mistake of not realizing how seriously she took this dog sled racing.

What was there about her that made it so imperative he erase that frown? Jenna wasn't conventionally pretty—especially not at the moment, with her assertive chin thrust so belligerently at him—but he couldn't seem to get enough of looking at her.

Tonight she was wearing her blond hair in a soft chignon, with wispy curls framing her face. Her pale blue wool dress clung to the high breasts and pleasantly curved hips of a more-than-adequate figure. Not as sexy as a California beach girl at first glance but more provocative to him. He knew he had to touch her, hold her, caress her, that he'd never be satisfied until he could make love to her—a somewhat remote possibility. With her fanatic interest in dog sledding, once she discovered his sin of omission plus the incipient sin of commission to follow, he'd be stone cold dead in the market as far as she was concerned.

Unfortunately, she might find out the truth about the dogs at any time. He didn't want to rush things with this woman, who was so worth savoring. At the same time, he didn't like his position. He really ought to tell her and take the consequences.

How the hell had he gotten himself into this predicament?

Weylin leaned toward her. "What does one do for winter recreation here besides racing dog sleds?" he asked.

"Skiing. Tobogganing. Ice skating." Her words were clipped. "Or, there's hot-air ballooning if you prefer more of a spectator sport."

"Ballooning? In this cold?"

"A hot-air balloon doesn't care whether it's warm or cold. Besides, they use less propane in the winter."

"I think I prefer the more traditional winter sports. I've skied and tobogganed in the California mountains."

"But never ice skated?"

He shook his head.

She eyed him speculatively. "Why?"

"I always figured ice skating was one of those things you had to learn as a child, and I didn't. There must have been indoor rinks in Los Angeles, but I never noticed. With the ocean and all the sunshine..." He shrugged.

The corners of her mouth turned up slightly. "I can picture you as a teenager on a surfboard searching for the perfect wave."

"There's no such thing. I gave up surfing for sailboats. Now, there's a challenge."

Jenna began eating her salad. "Ice skating's a challenge too. Of course, if you don't think you can..."

"I can do anything I set my mind to."

Her smile broadened. Damn it, she was teasing him.

"What I meant was," she went on, "if you don't *want* to learn to skate—"

"Just try me!"

"Tomorrow?"

Weylin thought a moment. "I'm meeting with the lawyers in the morning. In the afternoon I have a conference. I wanted to ask if you'd have lunch with me though."

Jenna, seemingly on the verge of refusing, suddenly grinned. "Thank you," she said sweetly, "but only if you agree to let me choose the place. I'll come by and pick you up too. I insist."

What's she up to, he wondered. Never mind, he really didn't care where or what they ate, as long as she was with him. For a moment there he'd been convinced she was going to turn him down. He didn't have much time scheduled for this Alaskan trip—a week at the outside—and every day counted.

Why has this woman become so important to you, Matthews? he asked himself, studying the glow of amusement in her velvety eyes.

. A challenge, that's what Jenna Henderson was. A real challenge. One he was determined to meet. Jenna hummed to herself as she guided her red Toyota through the crowded noontime streets. She wasn't quite sure if the tune was "The Blue Danube" or "The Skater's Waltz," but it didn't matter. Either was appropriate.

Weylin had asked her to pick him up on E Street, in front of his lawyers' offices. She turned off Third and spotted him immediately, city elegant in a gray topcoat and no hat. Luckily, she'd anticipated that and brought earmuffs. Doing her best to ignore her speeding pulse—assuring herself it was only because she could hardly wait for his reaction to her lunch plans—Jenna pulled to the curb.

"Damn, this is a cold city," Weylin said as he ducked into the car. "Doesn't the sun ever get any higher than that?" He gestured toward the red noontime sun, low in the sky.

"The sun never is high this far north, and in December we're getting close to the shortest day in the year, when we get less than five hours of sunlight."

"End of the world," Weylin muttered.

"Almost. Isn't it exciting?"

"If you say so." He smiled at her, his gaze approving the fit of her emerald-green wool pants and jacket.

Jenna smiled back. The sudden warmth suffusing her, she told herself, wasn't because he sat next to her, nor was it from his smile or the secret message in those green eyes. It was anticipation.

"Where are we headed?" he asked.

"Out Northern Lights Boulevard. It's a surprise."

She glanced sideways at him. He wore no scarf and under his topcoat she noticed a blue and maroon striped tie that complemented his dark blue suit. Conservatively appropriate for business meetings but...She bit her lip to keep from laughing.

Ahead of her the Chugach range thrust snow-covered peaks into the deep blue of the sky, making her momentarily long to be with the dogs on a wilderness trail far from the city's congestion. Yet she wouldn't miss the next few hours for anything.

After last night's dinner, Weylin had suggested dancing but she'd refused. She'd also been prepared to refuse a kiss when he said good-night to her at her apartment door. To her surprise, all he'd done was brush her cheek with his fingertips and turn away. Unconsciously she lifted her gloved fingers to her cheek as she remembered, then quickly returned her hand to the wheel when she realized what she was doing. She was in command and she intended to stay that way.

"How long do you have?" she asked Weylin.

He glanced at his watch. "Until two."

"Wonderful. That gives us plenty of time." She slanted another look at him and found him watching her speculatively.

"Isn't your apartment out this way?"

Jenna nodded, not trusting herself to speak. Did he really expect…? Oh, this was getting better and better.

There was far less snow in Anchorage than there had been in the Chugaches, and when Jenna pulled off the boulevard onto the access road at Goose Lake, she saw the glint of ice and nodded. She hadn't checked the lake ahead of time, but the ice had been clear of snow the week before, and less than an inch had fallen since. Pulling into the plowed parking lot, she stopped the car.

Weylin stared at the spruce-ringed lake where ten or so people were skating on the ice, then turned to her, eyebrows raised.

"I borrowed a pair of skates for you," she told him. "I think they'll fit well enough." She gestured toward the back seat. "I brought heavy socks, mitts, and earmuffs." She pulled on a green-and-white stocking cap and reached for her own skates.

Weylin caught her arm. "You expect me to ice skate?" He looked down at his topcoat. "In this?"

"'Just try me,' you said." Jenna did her best to look innocent. "I didn't think it would matter to you what you wore."

"Some surprise."

She widened her eyes. "Too much of a challenge for you?"

Releasing her, Weylin twisted around for the skates and other gear. When he turned back she saw he was grinning ruefully. "You really hooked me, but good. I see I'll have to be careful of you tricky Alaskans."

Once on the ice, Weylin was as wobbly at first as a nearby toddler on his tiny double-bladed skates.

"Come on, Tommy, you're doing fine," the child's mother coaxed. She skated backward ahead of the boy, who stumbled toward her, arms flailing wildly.

Jenna skated in circles around Weylin. "Want me to help?" she asked him, her voice choked with suppressed laughter. He cut a truly incongruous figure, with his striped tie visible at the V of his topcoat, staggering so determinedly along the ice. He wore the mitts but had left the earmuffs behind.

"I think I'm getting into the swing of it," he called back.

To her amazement, she saw that he was. Though his ankles still turned in, he'd begun to do a creditable glide. He was definitely a quick learner. Jenna skated closer and, crossing her arms, reached for his hands.

"I'll skate with you. This is the way to hold on."

A few turns and one fall later, Weylin had improved remarkably. Exhilarated by the exercise, the crisp, clean air, and Weylin's company, Jenna released him and executed a graceful figure eight, ending up at his side.

"You know, you're really—" She broke off abruptly when she saw a man with a camera standing on the bank near them.

"I'm from the *Alaskan News*," the khaki-jacketed man holding the camera said. "I'd like to snap a few shots, if you don't mind." His eyes were on Weylin, taking in the topcoat and tie.

Weylin came to a wobbly stop and started to shake his head. The chance was too good to miss, Jenna decided.

"Mr. Matthews is from California," she cut in hastily. "First time on skates, first time in Alaska. He wants to sample everything we have to offer."

Weylin scowled at her, and she smiled mockingly back at him.

"Way to go, man," the reporter said, lifting his camera.

For an instant Jenna thought Weylin was going to grab the camera, but then she saw him take a deep breath, gathering control.

"Ms Henderson plans to show me everything," Weylin said. "With her I intend to capture the entire Alaskan experience." He reached for Jenna and drew her close to his side. "We've already mushed the trails together, and today we're skating. Tomorrow, who knows? Skiing or tobogganing, possibly. After that—" he paused and grinned at the newsman "—well, there must be a few Alaskan indoor sports Ms Henderson can teach me."

Held so tightly against Weylin she couldn't move, Jenna thought quickly. "Mr. Matthews is talking about hackey-sack," she managed finally. "He's never heard of it and, of course, I wouldn't dream of letting him return to California until he becomes a hackey-sack expert."

"Great. Could I get a shot of you skating, Mr. Matthews?" the reporter asked.

After the newsman was gone, Jenna could no longer contain her laughter. "You'll make tomorrow's morning paper for sure," she crowed. "Oh, it was beautiful. I haven't enjoyed anything so much in years. The look on your face, Weylin. If you could have seen—"

"I probably will see it—in the morning paper. That's two I owe you, and don't think I'll forget." He began to laugh. "I thought you were the soul of propriety, but it's obvious you can't be trusted."

He caught her by her upper arms, staring down at her. The glint in his eyes set off an answering spark inside her that started her heart trip-hammering in her chest. A moment later neither of them was laughing.

"You remind me of a dryad in that green jacket," he murmured. "A winter dryad, as elusive as a snowflake. But I've captured you now." He bent his head, his lips nearing hers.

As she felt the white mist of his breath on her face, her spiraling eagerness for his kiss panicked her. She tried to jerk free, forgetting she was on skates.

Her feet slid out from under her, and Jenna clutched at Weylin for balance, only to upset him. Down they tumbled onto the ice, arms and legs entangled. Jenna found herself on her back with Weylin half atop her.

"Are you okay?" he asked.

She nodded, expecting him to move and help her up. Instead he thrust a mittened hand under her head and pulled her to him. She had no time to protest as his lips covered hers, warm and demanding, melting any resistance she might have mustered.

Her consciousness of the hard, cold ice beneath her faded; she no longer heard the scrape of other skaters' blades or the rumble of traffic on Northern Lights Boulevard. She dissolved into this kiss, aware of nothing except Weylin, his arms, his lips. The taste of him tantalized her tongue.

When she was younger she'd fantasized about a kiss from a dream lover that would change her life forever. The urgent reality of Weylin's mouth on hers was far more arousing than any fantasy. Tremors of desire raced through her body, and her lips parted to take him in, to consume him.

She heard the rasp of his quickened breath, felt his arms tighten as their kiss deepened. She clung to him, yearning to be closer, closer, closer...

When he pulled away slightly, Jenna moaned in protest, her eyes fluttering open to meet his. Green fire blazed at her.

"If hackey-sack's anything like this, I can hardly wait to play," Weylin murmured.

Three

———

Weylin watched Jenna unpack her picnic basket, which rested on a table in the new and modern student union of the University of Alaska, just the other side of Goose Lake.

"Homemade cream of broccoli soup," she said, pouring the steaming liquid out of an insulated container into heavy plastic mugs. "And I made reindeer sausage sandwiches to go with it."

The soup was excellent, but Weylin eyed his wheatbread sandwich with suspicion before taking his first bite. To his surprise he enjoyed the pungent flavor.

"Good," he told her, reaching for a second sandwich. "Never ate reindeer meat before."

"Even the broccoli is Alaskan grown," she said. "One of my friends had a garden last summer. With the extra summer sunlight, vegetables and flowers do really well."

"I take it hackey-sack is homegrown too. An indoor game, you said. You haven't told me how to play it."

She glanced at him from under her lashes, her brown eyes bright with mischief. "Oh, hackey-sack can be played indoors or out—at least in the summer. I'd rather show than tell."

Weylin's pulses leaped with anticipation. The feel of Jenna in his arms, the taste of her, the warmth of her response, were addictive. Already he needed more. And soon.

"Tonight?" he suggested.

She shook her head. "I'm taking the dogs for a fifteen-mile run, and I won't be back before midnight. Tomorrow's Saturday—how about the afternoon, at my apartment?"

"Sounds good."

"You could, um, dress more casually. It's not a formal game. In fact, hackey-sack can get quite strenuous."

The bright green of her jacket deepened the brown of her eyes. She'd tied some of her hair back with a matching green ribbon, and the rest spilled in blond curls onto her shoulders. He wondered if she had any idea how enticing she looked or how much he longed to hold her again. Now. Right here.

"About one, then," he said, hearing the rasp in his voice and wondering how he was going to wait that long.

He arrived on Jenna's doorstep the next day promptly at one. She opened the door, smiling. He resisted the impulse to put his arms around her and pull her to him. No need to rush it, he cautioned himself. As he started to greet her, he thought he heard a man's voice and looked past her, frowning.

"The others got here early," she said demurely. "Come in and meet them."

Weylin advanced into the living room, doing his best to conceal his disappointment as he realized he should have suspected Jenna might be teasing him again.

Two couples greeted him—Len and Trina and Joe and Emily. Both men were bearded and Joe, the taller, also had a bushy mustache. Len, square built and balding, was overweight. If they all were hackey-sack players, Len was probably less of a threat than Joe, depending on how athletic the game was.

Weylin found neither of the women as attractive as Jenna. Emily's voluptuous curves showed to advantage in a blue velour jogging suit, but neither she nor Trina were Jenna, trim and uncluttered in jeans and blue T-shirt with an "Alaska, the Last Frontier" slogan across the front in red.

She'd furnished her apartment sparsely, using Danish modern in pale woods and chrome. Beautifully clean lines, like Jenna herself. Today she wore her hair pulled back into a single braid down her back, with tendrils escaping to curl around her face. He shook his head at her, grinning wryly, then turned to the men.

"Jenna tells me hackey-sack is Alaska's number-one indoor sport," he said. "Can that be right?" Out of the corner of his eye he saw her flush.

Len just smiled, while Joe seemed to ponder the question.

"Hackey-sack's better outside," Joe said finally, "but winter gear's too hampering."

"If we're going to play," Trina put in, "we'd better secure the lamps and loose bric-a-brac. It'll get wild once we get going."

As the women began moving table lamps, Len plucked something from his pocket and flipped it at Weylin, who lifted a quick hand and caught it.

A ball, made of what looked like deerskin, with stitching between the pieces of hide making up the cover. Small, about the same size as a handball but nothing like it in consistency. This felt almost as yielding as a beanbag but was packed more tightly.

Weylin tossed the ball into the air a few times to gauge the heft. "What's inside?" he asked.

"Beats me," Len said.

"Polyethylene pellets," Jenna answered. "I looked once."

"Not when the Indians made them," Trina added. "Hackey-sacks come from the Indians. I think they used evergreen needles. Or maybe dried corn, if they had it."

"The point of the game is to keep the hackey-sack in the air," Len said. "You can hit it with your elbows, head, knees, feet, hips, whatever, as long as you don't touch the ball with your hands. Hands are not allowed."

"How do you figure the winner?" Weylin asked.

Len shrugged. "There isn't a winner. Like I said, we try to keep the ball in the air as long as we can, passing it from person to person in the circle. Makes no difference who it goes to or how you get it there, as long as you don't use hands."

Weylin glanced at Jenna. Among other omissions, she hadn't mentioned you couldn't win at hackey-sack. Len was wrong though. It was obvious the one who was best at keeping the ball up would be the winner.

"Ready any time you are," Weylin said, smiling.

A few minutes later, he realized he'd underestimated Len, who was not only very well coordinated but an expert hackey-sack player. Weylin had fumbled a few tosses to begin with, but soon got into the rhythm of the game and was doing okay.

Up with the foot, out with the hip, bounce it off the head to the next player.

"Going great, man," Len called to him. "Keep it up—we'll set a record."

Weylin felt the familiar rush of adrenaline as he flung himself into competition. He'd always been good at sports; with a little practice he'd be better at this than Len, and Len was easily the best of the group, though Jenna ran him a close second.

The next time he played this game he'd be the best.

"Hackey-sack's for fun," Jenna said to Weylin in the kitchen later, after the others had left.

"I *had* fun," he said.

She raised her eyebrows. To her, Weylin had looked tense and driven.

"I enjoyed the game," he insisted. "I liked your friends."

"We're all taking a canoe trip down the Yukon River next summer." The trip would be even more exciting if Weylin joined them, she thought....

Jenna broke off her musing and plugged in the coffee maker. No, it wouldn't be possible. She was building too quickly on a flimsy foundation. One kiss on the ice meant nothing, not to a man like Weylin. She drew in her breath as he caught her around the waist from behind.

"Jenna," he murmured, his lips close to her ear.

She closed her eyes, leaning back against him, feeling the hardness of his body pressing against hers. His hands slid up under her breasts, not quite cupping them. Delicious streamers of desire fluttered through her.

How she longed to give way to her impulses, to forget everything except Weylin and the passion he aroused in her. No man had ever affected her like this—it was as though he had the ability to draw a charmed circle about the two of them so that the rest of the world was shut away and nothing mattered but the moment. All the plans she'd made before she met him paled into insignificance when he held her in his arms.

The dogs. The Iditarod. They weren't insignificant.

Jenna took a deep, shuddering breath and exhaled raggedly, stiffening in Weylin's embrace. She'd worked long and hard for the chance to show her ability as a trainer. It was the most important thing in her life.

Wasn't it?

She eased from Weylin's arms and turned to face him. "How long will you be in Anchorage?" It came out more bluntly than she wished, but that didn't matter; she had to know.

"I have to straighten out Maki Equipment before I can think of leaving."

"You're equivocating."

"So I am." He half-smiled. "I'd have sworn I'm not the type. Does it really matter, Jenna?" His green eyes were bright with his need for her.

"It matters to me." She couldn't explain herself any more clearly than that. He'd probably laugh at her if she told him she'd waited twenty-three years for the right man and, no matter how she longed for his touch, she doubted he was that man.

She wanted—no, needed—someone who believed in commitment, not in passing fancies. Someone who loved dogs, who loved Alaska. A man who could relax and enjoy himself instead of always competing.

Weylin shrugged, his eyes turning opaque. "I'll be in Anchorage ten more days at the outside."

How could she explain? Having him standing so close to her made her knees weak, made her want what he wanted. He must know that from the wild throbbing of the pulse in her throat and her uneven breathing. Yet somehow she had to tell him it would be better if they didn't see each other again.

"What's the matter, Jenna?" His fingers stroked her cheek. "You can't deny what's between us; I know you feel it."

She swallowed. "Yes, I feel it."

He reached for her and she backed away, coming up against the counter. "You don't understand," she said, gasping. "There's the dog team, the race..."

"What in hell does the race have to do with us?"

"To me it means everything. You don't know how much I want to run the Iditarod—I have to make you understand. Don't—don't loom over me. I can't think when you do that."

Weylin took a step back, frowning.

"If I run the big race," she went on, "it really doesn't matter whether I come in number one or not. I'd like to, naturally, but that's not the point. I won't be the first woman to run the Iditarod, far from it.

Still, women are in the minority on that run and once I finish the Iditarod, everyone who matters will know how good a trainer I am. All trainers have to prove themselves—especially one who is a woman.''

Jenna straightened up. "I think I'm doing an excellent job with Mr. Maki's dogs; they weren't even a team when I started. You say you like challenges—well, that's what it is for me. It's a challenge to take fourteen dogs and weld them into a sled team, perhaps capable of winning the Iditarod. I really think they might. Come blizzard or thaw, I'm going to run the Iditarod, and nothing's going to stop me."

"Letting me hold you is going to make a difference?''

Her lips quivered. "I—I'm afraid so. You're not like anyone else. There's a—I don't know, a strange allure. What if—"

She stopped, unable to go on. *What if we make love and then you leave me and I'm not the same? Not the calm and collected Jenna who can put everything into training the dogs. What if you take part of me with you?*

"Running the Iditarod is the most important thing in my life," she finished.

She had to break off with him while she still was in control of herself. Once Weylin was gone she'd soon forget him. Wouldn't she?

"You're telling me the race is more important than you and me?" Weylin growled.

Jenna chewed on her lip. "There's no future for you and me."

"How the hell do you know?" He grasped her shoulder, anger flaring in his eyes. "Even if it turns out there isn't, how can you throw away the chance to find out? For no good reason."

"There *is* a good reason. You just don't understand."

"Dogs. Races." He scowled. "Those damn dogs belong to the company—Maki made them part of the assets before he sold out. The dogs belong to Whittaker Enterprises, Jenna, and they're going to be sold."

She wrenched away from him. "I don't believe you!"

"Maki never got around to telling you what he did, but it's true, all right. That's why I trekked into the damn wilderness after you, to bring the dogs back where they belonged."

Jenna stared at him, appalled, feeling as though she'd been stabbed through the heart. She had to believe him; Weylin had no reason to lie.

"You—you're going to sell the dogs?"

"I explained company policy to you the night we met. Whittaker Enterprises strips off the frills. The dogs aren't necessary, don't contribute; they cost money to feed, train, and vet."

Rage began to simmer inside Jenna. "You knew!" she cried. "You planned to sell the dogs from the very beginning, but you didn't tell me. You let me go on believing I'd continue to train them, let me plan on the Iditarod. You let me make a fool of myself."

"Jenna, I'm sorry."

"Why didn't you tell me?"

"Out there in the mountains didn't seem to be the time or place, and then—well, what there is between us kept me from admitting the truth. I didn't want to hurt you."

She wanted to explode, to scream at him, pound him with her fists, order him from her sight. How could he do such a thing? She hated him, hated him, hated him!

With an immense effort, Jenna held back. Keep your head, she cautioned herself. Count to ten. The dogs aren't sold yet. Maybe Weylin will listen to reason.

"Did it ever occur to you," she said as calmly as she could, "that the value of the dog team will increase ten times or more if it wins the Iditarod?"

Weylin blinked at her.

"Even a second- or third-place team's value goes up. In fact, if the dogs come in among the first ten, you'll get more money for them than you will if you sell them now, when they're not even completely trained."

"I take your point, but—"

"Chingo's an outstanding leader, and Sonia runs him a close second. If Chingo weren't the alpha male she might even surpass him; she's the alpha female and has a lot of potential."

"Alpha—what's alpha?"

Jenna relaxed a little. He was listening at least. "There's always a dominant dog in every pack, as well as a dominant bitch. They're called alphas and usually make good leaders because the other dogs obey them, follow them, look to them to set the pace. Of course, the ultimate leader of every dog team has to be the musher who drives them. Otherwise the lead dog won't obey, and if he or she doesn't, none of the other dogs will.

"Chingo's leadership qualities can make the team a winning combination." If Chingo doesn't continue to defy me, she said to herself. No reason to mention that at the moment. She'd find a way to bring Chingo to heel.

If she got the chance.

Weylin sighed. "I can't deny you make a good case, but policy is policy. Whittaker got where it is by hewing to the line. The dogs aren't necessary to the business, and they'll be sold before I leave Anchorage."

She stared at his closed face, at the stubborn lines around his mouth, and despaired. Hatchet man, she'd called him, and it was obvious he took his job to heart. She'd never get him to bend, to give even a fraction of an inch.

"You should have told me in the beginning," she repeated.

"I...couldn't."

"Because you didn't want to hurt me?" Her eyes narrowed. "I don't believe you. Surely you realized the hurt would be greater the longer you kept quiet. There was another reason, wasn't there?" Her voice rose. "You wanted to romance me, and you figured you wouldn't be able to once I knew about the dogs. Admit it—that was your cheap, shabby reason."

"Jenna, listen to—"

"I despise you!" she cried. "I never want to see you again."

Weylin grasped her shoulders. "Damn it, listen! I was wrong, I admit it, but I won't have you belittling the reason. What's between us is powerful, wonderful. I feel it. You feel it. There's nothing cheap and shabby about it."

Fury blazed up in her, and she fought to free herself from his grip. "All you think about is winning." She spat the words at him. "Even in a game where no one wins, like hackey-sack. You saw me the same way. A challenge to overcome, to win." Still held by his fingers digging into their flesh, she glared at him. "You listen to *me*. I can't ever be won. I'm not a prize, I'm a woman with free choice, and I'd never choose you. Never. Let me go, get out of my apartment, my life. Now and forever."

Instead, he pulled her to him, his mouth coming down on hers, hard and demanding. He crushed her against him, and she felt his urgent desire. Even while she struggled to free herself, her traitorous body responded to Weylin's embrace, and she had to fight herself as well as him.

Part of her wanted to surrender, to lose all control, to give free rein to the demanding passion that quickened her blood. She detested him, but at the same time he stirred her as no man ever had, infused her with a savage hunger for him.

Jenna wrenched her mouth from his. "No!" she cried.

Still he gripped her, his eyes hot and feral, glaring into hers. She couldn't breathe, couldn't think.

"No," she said again, the word a whisper.

"I don't give up easily." His voice was husky. "I hear your words, but I feel what you really want. Your need is as great as mine, isn't it?" When she didn't answer, his lips drew back, exposing his teeth. "Isn't it?"

Jenna gathered her wits together. She'd never admit how he made her feel. "All I want from you is for you to leave." Her tone was low, her words quivered with outrage. "I'd rather a real wolf had stalked from the trees that night than you."

Weylin blinked, his hands easing, and she yanked herself free. Her chest heaved as she tried to catch her breath, her eyes never leaving his, even though she didn't fear him, only herself.

Weylin stepped back. He nodded slightly. "Have it your way Jenna. For now." He turned on his heel, snatching up his jacket as he passed through the living room. She followed slowly, warily.

With one hand on the doorknob, he half turned. "By the way, I'll expect you to go on taking care of the dogs until they're sold."

Before she had a chance to answer, he was out the door and gone. Jenna sank into the nearest chair. She'd outfaced him, and she'd come out ahead.

It was only a skirmish though. The war was already lost. There was no way to keep him from selling her dogs.

Four

For a week Jenna brooded, avoiding her friends and seeing only the dogs during daily runs. She dreaded to hear the phone ring. It might be Weylin, and she couldn't refuse to take a call from him because he might be phoning to say he'd sold the dogs. But it was never him. Nor did he come to her apartment.

One week ran into two. If anything, her spirits drooped even lower. She missed him and was angry because she did. How could you miss a man you loathed?

When the phone rang on Sunday morning, Jenna told herself it wouldn't be him but couldn't repress a flicker of disappointment when she heard Emily's voice.

"We're all going skating this afternoon—how about joining us?"

"No, thanks, Em. I just don't feel like skating."

"Too busy with the handsome *cheechako*?"

"No!" The word exploded from Jenna.

After a tiny silence Emily said, "You want to talk about it?"

"There's nothing much to say. I wish I'd never set eyes on him."

"That bad, huh?"

"Oh, Em, he's going to sell the dogs. I didn't know it, but they belong to the company, not to Mr. Maki."

"Oh God, that's a real downer. What are you going to do about it?"

"What can I do? The dogs aren't mine."

"Hey, I thought you were a fighter. Can't you convince Weylin to change his mind?"

"Hatchet men don't change their minds."

"Well, how about Mr. Maki—can't you ask him to talk to Weylin?"

"I thought of that, but Mr. Maki took his wife to Hawaii for the holidays. It'll be too late by the time he returns. Anyway, Weylin's so closed-minded. 'Company policy'; that's all his tape plays."

"I remember once when I was working at Harper Hospital in Portland. You wouldn't believe the monster of a supervisor on the surgical ward. I won't go into the miserable details, but she didn't like me and saw to it that I had the least desirable days off and all the worst work.

"Hospitals really hate nurses who don't go through channels, but I figured what did I have to lose except a rotten job? I knew a phone call would get me nowhere, so I bypassed the supervisor and went in person to the director of nurses. The next day I was transferred to pediatrics, a dream wing. Going to the head honcho paid off for me."

When Jenna said nothing, Emily added, "So much for my shady past in the lower Forty-eight. How about reconsidering the skating?"

"Sorry, another time." Jenna hesitated and then went on. "By the way, if I decide to go out of town for a few days, would you and Joe look after the dogs? Take them for runs and all?"

"Love to. Joe's convinced Chingo's got a higher I.Q. than some of the men he works with. He'll enjoy mushing your team. Where are you going?"

"Whittaker, the outfit that took over Maki's, is based in L.A. After listening to you I'm thinking of flying down."

"I'm glad I could help. Listen, wear your hair down and a blue Alice-in-Wonderland-type dress, and you'll melt the old tycoon's heart. Or if it's a woman, she'll feel motherly."

Jenna smiled for the first time in days. "Somehow I don't think Alice-on-the-trail is exactly the right image."

"Maybe not. I have an Eskimo *kuspak* you can wear if you think that's more appropriate."

"I'll take my chances with what I've got. Thanks for calling. You've made me feel that I've got a chance."

"Weylin's still a hunk, closed mind and all."

"Him I'm definitely going to forget I ever knew."

"Lots of luck."

After Emily said good-bye, Jenna dialed a travel agency, afraid that if she waited to think it over she'd lose her nerve. But, as Emily had said, what did she have to lose?

Jenna stared at the red-haired woman behind the car rental desk at International Airport in Los Angeles. "You have what kind of condition?"

The redhead smiled. "Oh, I forgot, you're a foreigner. A Santa Ana condition means we have hot winds blowing off the desert. Just in time for Christmas; it happens every year."

Jenna shed her tan suit jacket as she left the terminal. The down coat she carried seemed to trap the heat and channel it along her body. Her gold blouse was long sleeved, and she unbuttoned the cuffs and folded them back as soon she climbed behind the wheel of her rental car.

The blue compact wasn't equipped with air-conditioning, so Jenna rolled down the windows before studying the map of the freeway system. The redhead had traced her route in blue from International Airport to Anaheim, where Whittaker Enterprises was located. Getting there looked simple enough. She checked her watch. Three-thirty. She ought to make the drive in plenty of time to visit the company before five.

What the woman at the rental counter hadn't thought to tell Jenna was how quickly she had to make up her mind about which way she wanted to go after reading the green freeway signs. Or how difficult it was to find her way back to the right place once she had missed a turnoff. Or the nightmare that rush-hour traffic could be.

Jenna pulled into the outskirts of Anaheim at five-thirty, frazzled and sweaty. Weylin had told her she'd prefer California to Alaska once she visited there. He must have been out of his mind.

She certainly didn't want to think about Weylin, or even about Whittaker Enterprises. All she wanted at the moment was a motel where she could find a shower and a cold drink.

Jenna fell asleep early in the air-conditioned motel room and dreamed she was on a snowy Alaskan trail with her dogs. She'd stopped for the night and was staking the team. Chingo resisted.

"Don't be stubborn," she warned the lead dog as she hauled him toward the chain. He dug in his feet and refused to move. Jenna crouched and glared into his slanting dark eyes, watching with disbelief as the eyes changed to yellow-green, as Chingo's black coat lightened to a silver gray.

Another trick, she told herself. He's pretending to be a wolf to scare me. I'll show him!

She grabbed the animal by the scruff of the neck, exerting all her strength to drag him to the picket line. She couldn't budge him. Suddenly he twisted, catching her off balance so that she tumbled into the snow. Then he was on her, growling, his green eyes aflame with menace.

Only he wasn't Chingo. He wasn't a wolf either. Weylin held her in a fierce embrace, pinioning her so she couldn't move. She gasped in shock as he tightened his grip.

Where were her clothes? She felt the chill of the snow on the bare flesh of her back, and all the while Weylin's face came closer and closer, blotting out the light. She could see nothing but the fiery brilliance of his eyes, bright points of phosphorescence that mesmerized her.

Once his lips touched hers she'd be doomed. She'd be his forever, and together they'd run under the moon. She longed for his kiss even as she feared it.

She was cold, so cold...

Jenna sat up, shivering. The sheet and blanket had slipped to the floor, and her shortie nightgown was little protection against the chill of the air-conditioning. She stumbled from the bed and shut it off.

Damn the man. He even haunted her dreams.

By morning the room was all too warm, and Jenna shook her head as she looked over the clothes she'd brought. She hadn't expected L.A. to be really cold in December, but she certainly hadn't counted on 100-degree temperatures. The short-sleeved white cotton sweater with the brown skirt were the lightest-weight clothes she'd packed.

She braided her thick blond hair and coiled the braid at the back of her head to keep her neck cool.

"You have beautiful hair," Weylin had told her, smoothing a strand between his fingers....

No, no, no. He was out of her life and she'd keep him out of her thoughts. Wouldn't it be fun, though, to see the look on Weylin's face if she managed to convince the head of Whittaker Enterprises she was right about the dogs?

No emotion, she warned herself. You'll present only facts. Show Mr. Whittaker the value of dogs who've run the Iditarod, compared with the value of dogs who haven't competed. You have it down in black and white; any reasonable man will at least look at the figures you've compiled.

All you have to do is get in to see Jarvis Whittaker.

The company buildings were easy to find. Jenna parked the compact in a visitor's slot, took a deep breath of the dry, hot desert air, and headed for the main entrance.

"Mr. Whittaker, please," she said to the receptionist, hoping her tone sounded crisper than she felt.

"Mr. Whittaker?" The dark-skinned young woman frowned at Jenna.

"Yes, the president. I'm Jenna Henderson. I've flown here from Anchorage, Alaska, to see him, and it's most important that I do."

"I'm sorry, but Mr. Whittaker—"

"Tell him I've come about Maki Equipment, his new company."

"I can't tell Mr. Whittaker anything, Ms Henderson. He's not here."

Jenna's heart sank. "When will he be back?"

The receptionist shook her head. "You have the wrong name."

"Jarvis Whittaker is listed as president of Whittaker Enterprises. Isn't he in charge of the company?"

"No, Ms Henderson."

"Then who is in charge?"

"I am," a familiar voice said from the other side of the reception area.

Jenna whirled around, pulses pounding, to stare into Weylin Matthews's green gaze.

Weylin strode across the soft brown plush of the carpet and took her arm, guiding her toward an inner office. Once inside, he shut the door. She pulled her arm from his grasp, vaguely aware of a vast mahogany desk and other dark gleaming furniture.

"I thought you knew I headed the company," Weylin said. "When I heard you were catching a flight to L.A., I tried to stop you. I was too late, so I flew here myself. Please sit down." He waved at an arm-chair upholstered in wine velvet.

Jenna's hands curled into fists. "I didn't know. You let me think you were just—just a hatchet man. Like you let me think the dogs were Mr. Maki's."

"I didn't lie to you about this. Since everybody at Maki Equipment from Maki on down knew who I was, I sure as hell thought you did too. I'd never have let you go to the trouble and expense of coming here if I'd had any idea—"

"Why is Jarvis Whittaker listed as president?"

"Technically, he still is president. He's an elderly, ill man, and I've had power of attorney for the past five years. I make all the decisions. I run Whittaker."

Her lips tightened. "So when you talk about company policy, you mean *your* policy."

"Look, Jenna, I'm sorry about this misunder-standing. I swear it wasn't deliberate on my part. I'd have stopped you if I could have. I was pretty sure you wouldn't talk to me on the phone, so I went by the kennels to see you. Joe was feeding the dogs, and nat-urally I wondered why. He told me."

"Have you sold them yet?" Her tone was bitter.

"No. It's not as easy as I thought." He held out his hands palms out. "I'll fly you back to Anchorage any time you want to go. The company has a jet."

"I have my return ticket on Alaskan Air lines, thank you." Jenna's mind buzzed with confusion.

She couldn't trust him, not after he'd misled her about the dogs. Yet she wanted to be fair. She hadn't checked with anyone at Maki Equipment, and it could be true he'd thought she was aware of his position. If so, her flying to L.A. wasn't his fault. At least, not entirely.

"Surely you have time for lunch with me before your return flight," Weylin said.

He seemed genuinely apologetic, but she was wary. On the one hand she was upset about finding him there, and she still nursed her anger over the dogs. On the other, if she tried to be civil perhaps the trip wouldn't be a total loss. Over lunch she could discuss the dogs calmly, as she'd intended to do with Jarvis Whittaker. She could show Weylin the figures she'd brought. Her flight wasn't until the next day anyway.

"Yes, thank you," she said. "Lunch would be fine." Her stern gaze warned him not to take anything else for granted.

Weylin's silver-gray Mercedes had air-conditioning, Jenna noted. Obviously he not only preferred the best, he didn't deny himself. She watched his long fingers turn the wheel as he eased from the on ramp into heavy freeway traffic and remembered how those fingers had stroked her cheek, had outlined her lips and caressed her throat. She wanted to feel them touch her again.

No, she did not.

"December can be a great month here," he was saying. "This heat's unusual."

"I was told the Santa Ana winds blow near Christmastime every year."

He grinned. "Trying to catch me out? Yes, we usually do have a Santa Ana sometime in December, but these hot desert winds aren't the norm in Southern California. They're just a freak condition that happen once, maybe twice, a year. They never last long."

The mention of Christmas reminded Jenna that it was only three days away. "How can you stand never having snow for Christmas?" she asked.

"Maybe I will have snow this year."

She glanced sideways at him, eyebrows raised.

"I have unfinished business in Anchorage."

No, she admonished herself as her breath caught, he doesn't mean you, he means selling the dogs. Keep your mind on what you're here for.

"Do you have a family?" she asked. "Someone to be with at Christmas?"

"Besides Grandpa Sam, no. And he expects me when he sees me. How about you?"

"Last year I flew back to Minnesota, to my uncle's. He raised my brother and me. All the family was there." Jenna sighed, recalling how good it had been.

"And this year?"

She blinked. "I haven't made plans." The words were defensive—she didn't want to think about being alone at Christmas. She looked away from him, staring out the window at the cars, at the green freeway signs, feeling depression settle over her like a tundra fog.

She was startled from her gloomy reverie when Weylin said, "Almost there," and swung onto a ramp.

Minutes later he pulled the Mercedes into the parking lot of Long Juan Silver's.

"Best Mexican food in the area," he told her. "You do like Mexican food?"

She almost wished she didn't so that she could hand him a sharp no. Unfortunately she loved it. But he should have asked earlier. He was too used to having his own way.

Instead of the colorful piñatas she'd half expected to see hanging from the ceiling, Long Juan's decor theme was Aztec, with silver metallic masks, bright weavings, and murals of stylized gods and goddesses.

As she sipped her marguerita, Jenna studied Weylin's face. In the cool dimness of the restaurant, his expression was shadowed, but she thought he looked troubled, even sad. Despite her own problems, she felt a pang of concern, which she immediately tried to suppress. As far as she could tell, Weylin ought to be sitting on top of the world.

"I've made a real mess of things with you, haven't I?" he asked. "From the instant I saw you in that snow by the campfire, I wanted to be with you, learn more about you. I wanted you to like me, to be as interested in me as I was in you."

"Not telling me the truth was hardly the way to go about it."

He smiled wryly. "Worst decision I ever made. No wonder you question my credibility. Scout's honor, no more evasions, no more concealments. Deal?"

"*Were* you a boy scout?"

"All the way to my Eagle badge."

Even as a boy, she thought, he had advanced as far as he could. Scouting must have been more of a challenge than fun to him. Did he ever just relax and enjoy himself without trying to conquer something or somebody?

"I missed you like hell, Jenna."

Her heart doubled its beat as she gazed into his green eyes. He still had the power to arouse her, without even a touch. His need for her showed clearly in his eyes, evoking her own longing for him. Her breath quickened, and she leaned toward him.

He reached across the table and entwined his fingers with hers. Warmth engulfed her, as though he'd taken her into his arms rather than merely clasping her hand. Desire raced along secret inner trails, parting her lips, making her eyelids heavy.

"When you look at me like that you drive me out of my mind." Weylin's voice was husky.

Jenna's mind wasn't working too well either. The urgent demands of her body overwhelmed coherent thought. Weylin, her pulses pounded, Weylin, Weylin.

"Come with me," he said softly.

The words floated in Jenna's head. What did they mean? A yes might be a commitment to more than she dared give, despite her need. She took a deep breath and leaned back in her chair, forcing herself to look at a scowling Aztec god instead of Weylin.

"I want you to meet my grandfather," he said, releasing her hand.

She blinked. His voice had changed; had he also changed his mind? Or was this what he had intended to ask all along and she'd assumed too much?

"He lives in Julian. It's a few hours' drive from here," Weylin went on. "Julian's in the mountains and will be cooler. I want you to see more of California than Los Angeles. This state isn't all cities any more than Alaska is all mountains."

She wanted to go. Wanted to be with Weylin.

"My flight's tomorrow morning. I don't think I'd better—"

"Plenty of time. Better still, cancel and stay over. Grandpa Sam has plenty of room. He lives in an old ranch house all by himself. We could spend Christmas with him; then none of us would be alone."

"Oh, but I couldn't. The dogs, for one thing—"

"Joe's taking good care of them."

"But your grandfather—it isn't fair to drop in on him suddenly and—"

"He's the most hospitable man in the world. Lonely too, though he won't admit it. Jenna, it could be a wonderful Christmas. Every once in awhile, we even get snow in Julian."

"I couldn't."

"You could. What harm would it do? Grandpa will welcome you, I want to be with you, and Christmas is coming. Good reasons, all of them."

I'd have three days to talk to Weylin about the dogs, she argued to herself. And it isn't as if I'm staying with *him* or I'm promising anything. Maybe if we spend time together he'll change his mind about the dogs. I've got new and convincing data he hasn't heard yet.

In the back of her mind a tiny voice warned her she was rationalizing. You want to be with Weylin, that's what it amounts to, Jenna, the voice insisted. Remember, Weylin is dangerous.

Well, what if I do happen to enjoy being with him? That isn't the point. If it weren't for the dogs I wouldn't even consider staying in California, not for a minute. And I can certainly take care of myself, so shut up, little voice, you don't know what you're talking about!

"I suppose I could change my flight reservation," she said tentatively.

While Jenna was still wondering if she was doing the right thing, Weylin whipped into action. The Mexican lunch they hadn't eaten was packed to go, a Whittaker employee was found to drive Jenna's rented car back to the airport, and then she and Weylin stopped at her motel so she could pick up her belongings and check out.

"You move fast," she said as she settled back into Weylin's car.

"I learned a long time ago that if I didn't, either people changed their minds or another person got what I wanted. Now I don't give anyone the chance to do either."

"Ruthless."

Weylin looked honestly surprised. "Not me. It's good business to know what you want and go after it with everything you've got. That's the way to win."

"And winning is all important?"

He glanced at her, frowning. "Well, isn't it?" His brow cleared. "Oh, you're thinking of that race you're so set on, the Iditarod. Be honest; if you did run it you'd really want to win, wouldn't you?"

"How can I deny that? What I've been trying to tell you, though, is that running the race, just being a part of it, is equally important to me. Come in first or not, I'd have accomplished what I set out to do."

Weylin shook his head. "I don't see it that way. If I ran it, I'd win."

Jenna smiled to herself at the notion of *cheechako* Weylin on the trail in early March, crossing frozen rivers, avoiding belligerent moose, mushing over Bering Sea ice. He'd never make it to Nome, much less win. Not that there was the slightest chance of him ever getting into the Iditarod to begin with. He didn't even like dogs, for a starter.

Should she begin discussing the Maki dogs now? Jenna shook her head. Not while he was fighting freeway traffic. She wanted his full attention, wanted to be able to show him facts and figures. She'd have to wait until they got to Julian.

Weylin pulled off at San Juan Capistrano, where they ate the Mexican food—tortillas, burritos, and tacos, along with fresh limeade—picnic style on the grounds of the old mission.

Jenna watched a sparrow as it hopped near her feet, hopeful for crumbs. She glanced about at the red-tiled adobe buildings surrounding an inner courtyard. "I thought there'd be swallows at Capistrano," she said.

"They've gone farther south for the winter. I don't know why; it seems warm enough here. At any rate, they'll be back in March, on the nineteenth. Want to wait?" He grinned at her.

She shot him a frown, relaxing in the shade of a pepper tree that seemed from its gnarled and gigantic trunk to be as old as the mission. The heat was enervating, but the bright sun filtering through the pepper tree's fringed leaves did raise her spirits. How different from the gloom of Alaska this time of the year. Yet that's where her heart remained, in that cold country.

"A few days of California is more than enough," she said.

"Wait until you've visited Julian. You'll feel right at home there—it even has abandoned gold mines."

Julian was another two hours away. After climbing the boulder-littered hills east of San Diego, they arrived in Julian near dusk. Weylin turned off onto a narrow blacktopped road that wound higher into the mountains, finally stopping at a drive blocked by a wooden gate. As he got out of the car to unfasten the gate, Jenna noticed the golden curve of the moon rising above the trees. At the same time she was startled to hear a howling that seemed to come from very close by.

She thrust her head from the open window. "I've heard California has coyotes," she called to Weylin, "but unless I'm greatly mistaken, that sounded like a wolf."

He said nothing, swinging the gate open but making no move to reenter the car. He glanced up at the moon instead of at her and threw his head back. From his throat rose a howl identical to the one she'd heard.

Hair rose on her nape as the sound echoed from the hills. She stared at Weylin in utter disbelief.

Werewolves didn't exist.

But what if he didn't know that?

Five

Old Lobo's welcoming me home," Weylin said as he slid behind the wheel of the Mercedes.

Jenna moistened her dry lips. "Lobo?"

Weylin nodded. "You were right—he's a wolf."

"You—you own a wolf?"

"No, Grandpa Sam does. Or Lobo owns him; I've never been sure which it is. They're like one person."

"Do you, uh, talk to Lobo often, like you did a minute ago?"

Weylin's teeth flashed white in the gathering darkness. "I learned wolf talk when I was a kid. We understand each other."

Jenna struggled to dismiss her mental picture of a young Weylin being taught by an aging man one day, a grizzled wolf the next. But she caught herself thinking how convenient it would have been if Weylin was a boy when his grandfather was a man, then a cub when the older man changed to—

Come on, she chided herself. How do you get into these weird fantasies, anyway? Weylin's grandfather is a man. Lobo's a wolf. Two entities, right? Certainly they're not one and the same.

As the car neared a two-story house, light suddenly poured onto the porch through an opened door.

"That you, Weylin?" a man shouted.

"Yes," Weylin called back. "I've brought a guest."

Moments later, Weylin led Jenna up wooden steps onto the wide porch and introduced her to a short and stocky man with white hair and a bushy white mustache.

Sam Matthews grasped her hand. "Welcome, Jenna," he said, drawing her inside. Weylin followed, shutting the door.

From behind another closed door at the opposite side of a long living room furnished in pine, Jenna heard a mournful whining.

"He knows it's you, boy," Sam said to Weylin.

Weylin strode across the room and flung the door open. A big gray animal sprang at him and Weylin dropped to his knees to hug the wolf. They rolled on the floor together, growling.

"Raised together," Sam said. "Practically litter mates."

Jenna couldn't get over Weylin's obvious joy at being with the wolf. And she'd thought he didn't like animals. She watched him get to his feet and urge Lobo toward her.

"This is my friend," Weylin said to the wolf. "Friend," he repeated.

Slowly, making no sudden movement, Jenna held out her hand, palm up, for Lobo to smell, treating him as she would a strange dog. Lobo sniffed her fingers, circled her once, then stared into her face with his slanted yellow-green eyes. The white on his muzzle marked him as aging.

"Lobo," she said softly. "Hello."

Apparently satisfied she was a friend, the wolf turned his back on her to nuzzle Weylin's hand.

"I was just thinking about supper," Sam said. "Got a couple of nice T-bones at the store today. How about it? You people hungry?"

"Let me help," Jenna offered, thinking that Sam was nothing like what she'd expected Weylin's grandfather to be. He seemed easygoing and relaxed, unlike his grandson.

"You can take charge of the salad," Sam told her. "Never did care for fiddling with lettuce. Weylin'll handle the coffee. Makes a better brew than me, and that's a fact."

By the time the meal was on the table, Jenna felt at home in Sam's house. More at home with Weylin too. He actually seemed to relax, something she hadn't seen him do till then.

The wolf, better mannered than many house dogs she'd known, lay quietly in the living room while they ate in a dining ell off the large country-style kitchen.

"Lobo's been well trained," she said.

"I raised him from a cub," Sam told her. "Bought his mother from a roadside zoo that went belly up, but she died bearing her litter. He was the only survivor. Talk about night feedings—that rascal demanded his milk every two hours night and day. He doesn't think of himself as different from me and Weylin. We're his pack and I'm the leader. So he does everything I tell him to do. That's inbred in a wolf, to obey the pack leader."

"The alpha male or female."

"Yeah, I read a book about that." Sam helped himself to more mashed potatoes. "Fellow made a lot of sense. That's the way it is with wolves."

"Dogs too. I train them, in Alaska."

"Do you now." Sam's hazel eyes studied her. "Always wanted to make a trip there. Maybe I will yet. Getting a mite crowded around Julian, new houses all over the place."

Sam kept a neat house, and the bedrooms were no exception. Jenna's room was wallpapered with yellow roses whose color had faded with age, but the white curtains at the windows were clean and crisp, and the bed linen on the white-painted iron bed not the least musty.

She looked out the window at the waxing moon and wondered why Weylin hadn't tried to kiss her when he showed her to the bedroom. She'd expected him to and had planned to coolly turn her head so his lips would only graze her cheek, then bid him a firm good-night. She felt let down because he'd made no attempt to touch her and, in fact, had said good-night first. She was disappointed to be cheated out of the satisfaction of turning away from his kiss.

There was absolutely no other reason for her disappointment.

Weylin lay in his old boyhood room, sleepless, unable to stop thinking about Jenna. There was more to her than he'd realized. Every time he was with her, he found her more fascinating, more desirable.

He wanted to be with her, not just for a night or two, a week or two—he needed her around him all the time. But how long was that really? He drew in a deep breath and let it out slowly. For as long as it lasted. Not that he was thinking of marriage. Good God, no, he wasn't ready for such a heavy commitment.

Maybe he'd never marry. It certainly didn't seem to work for at least half the people he knew, including his parents. Before his death, his father had failed at two marriages, among other things. And his mother? He detested his English stepfather because of the way he treated his mother and was angry at her for being so spineless. He hadn't been to London to see them in three years; he'd hardly call theirs a happy marriage.

Weylin was beginning to believe Jenna was one of the greatest challenges he'd ever faced. He was almost tempted to give in about those damn dogs. He wouldn't though. That would be the easy way; that would be cheating. Besides, he really believed in the policy he'd set for new acquisitions. No frills. Changing policy for no good reason had been a habit of his father's. It wasn't his father's worst failing, but it was one that hadn't helped the business. If his father had lived another year, not even a miracle could have saved Whittaker Enterprises. As it was, it had taken Weylin five years to build the company into the success it now was. No, he wouldn't change his policy.

Jenna would be his, but he wouldn't win her by keeping Maki's dogs. He visualized her down the hall in the room with the yellow roses on the walls. What did she wear to bed? Something silky and see-through? He smiled a little. Probably not; Jenna was practical, and Anchorage was cold.

Still, she knew California would be warm. What had she brought along to wear at night? Maybe nothing. The thought of her lying naked in a bed two rooms away from his made him groan. He could almost feel the warm softness of her skin under his hands, taste the sweetness of her mouth, smell the delicate, flowery perfume she wore, spiced by her own alluring scent.

If he went to her now...Weylin sat up in bed, excitement stirring in his loins. After a moment he sighed and stretched out again. Now wasn't the time, and he knew it. She was too defensive, not yet willing to admit she wanted him as much as he wanted her.

He had three days to convince her.

By the second day Jenna had decided Julian was situated in as charming an area as any she'd seen. She and Weylin had hiked miles through woods of pines, oaks, and hickories, with fallen leaves crackling underfoot. They'd startled coveys of quail and had even spotted two does. The abandoned gold mines and ruins of stamping mills reminded her of deserted mining settlements in Alaska.

Not that Julian was a ghost town. Far from it. Though small, it was full of spirit. New homes going up indicated growth, and several museums, one in a quaint old schoolhouse, were evidence of pride in the past. The only thing missing was snow; otherwise, the Christmas trees and lights along the turn-of-the-century main street were perfect.

But the Santa Ana lingered and, though the hot winds were weaker here in the mountains, the weather was still warm; too warm for a proper Christmas. Yet she had to admit she liked Julian. How could she help it? Looking at the Cuyamaca peaks to the south and Mount Palomar to the northwest almost made her feel as though she were home in Alaska.

On Christmas Eve, after they attended a candle-light service in the old Presbyterian church, Sam lit a fire in the stone fireplace of his living room, ignoring the weather. In the corner, a tall pine sparkled with ornaments and flashing lights. They drank eggnog to celebrate the season; then Sam took himself off to bed. The warm glow pervading Jenna wasn't entirely due to the fire and the brandy in the eggnog. She liked Sam, she liked Lobo. She liked...

No, "like" wasn't the right word for how she felt about Weylin. What was it? Attraction? Definitely. Desire? That too. But not love. Love was to be reserved for her dream man, the ideal one she'd spend the rest of her life with. Weylin wasn't that man. How could he be when they had not one single thing in common?

He sat beside her on a long, chintz-covered settee, the wolf asleep at his feet. Flames danced in his green eyes, reminding her of the night they met, the beginning of knowing him.

As if she'd spoken aloud, he glanced at her and said, "I think Lobo's the reason the dogs panicked when I walked into your night camp. I came here to see Grandpa before I left for Anchorage, and Lobo took a liking to the wolf fur on my new parka. I had a tough time convincing him it was mine, not his. He chewed it enough to leave his scent for your dogs."

"For one wild moment that night I thought you—" She paused, shaking her head. The brandy must be loosening her tongue.

Weylin leaned toward her. "What did you think?"

"Oh, it's silly. I heard a wolf howl, and I began re-calling old campfire tales about werewolves. Then you suddenly appeared out of nowhere and I—well, I didn't *really* think you were a werewolf, but..." She braced herself for his laughter.

He didn't even smile, only nodded thoughtfully.

"I've never told anyone," he said after a time, "but when I was eleven I tried very hard to turn myself into a wolf. I guess I knew I really couldn't, but still I hoped. It was before Lobo was born, before Grandpa bought his mother. I used to ride my bike from my parents' house in L.A. to the Griffith Park Zoo and stand outside the wolf den for hours wishing I could set them free to run in the hills, wishing I could run with them.

"Then I discovered an old book on magic that had a werewolf formula in it. I memorized the ritual and after months of searching, finally found a piece of wolfskin to make myself a belt, an essential part of the formula. You can't imagine my disappointment when, after following the ritual exactly, even to standing na-ked at a crossroads at midnight, I stayed human." Without looking at her, Weylin reached down and fondled Lobo's head.

Jenna couldn't think of anything to say. Weylin, the dynamic executive, the superachiever, admitting he'd once tried to change himself into a wolf? I don't imagine he's failed at much since then, she thought.

Why would a boy want to become an animal? He must have been unhappy. Certainly lonely, consider-ing he hadn't shared such a wonderful scheme with a friend. At eleven she'd had lots of friends and had shared everything.

Leaning back against the settee, Weylin turned to her and smiled a little. "So your feeling that night wasn't as silly as you thought. If I were mystically inclined I might say you sensed...something."

She continued to look at him, and he took her hand in his. "You did have every right to be frightened, alone at that night camp and suddenly seeing a stranger come out of the dark. An angry stranger, at that. I was so caught up in my own annoyance I never once thought of the effect I must have had on you."

"I recovered from the fright." She wished he hadn't touched her, yet she left her hand in his, hoping he wouldn't notice her too-rapid pulse.

If her fear that night had been easily overcome, the other effect he had on her had only gotten worse, gotten entirely out of her control.

Say good-night and go to bed, she told herself. You know that being alone with him is dangerous. You've spent two days here and you haven't brought up the supposed reason you came to Julian. Not once. Why? Because it was an excuse. You know he's not going to change his mind about the dogs, no matter what you say or do. You knew that when you agreed to come here. The real reason you're with him is because you want to be.

How big and dark the pupils of his eyes were. Wide and dark, like winter nights. Dark with desire.

She was so warm, from the weather and the fire and from her inner reaction to Weylin's unspoken demand. There was no mistaking what he wanted, and though he had only touched her hand, the pulsing surge of her response threatened to overwhelm her. Her resistance to him was breaking like river ice in the spring, and soon she'd be swept irresistibly along in the wild and passionate current only he could create.

Bon voyage!

No, the tiny voice in her head insisted, not with a man you can't trust. Not with a man who seeks only to win and ignores everything else. Not with a—

Weylin's lips brushed hers, silencing the voice. Kisses soft as cottonwood down touched her cheeks, her eyelids, her nose, before drifting along her throat to the hollow where her pulse throbbed in eager welcome.

The tip of his tongue outlined her lips, teasing them open. His teeth nipped gently at her lower lip. She leaned toward him and he shifted, semireclining in one corner of the settee and cuddling her against him, drawing her head down on his shoulder. Taking one of her hands, he turned it upward and, with his forefinger, traced a five-pointed design on her palm.

"A star?" she murmured, puzzled.

"A pentagram. I see it there. You know why, don't you?"

Weylin kissed her again, his lips no longer soft, driving the riddle of the pentagram from her mind. She held him to her, and the feel of the lithe strength of his body pressed to hers transmitted urgent messages deep within her, ones she understood and responded to without thinking.

His hand cupped her breast, warm through the cotton of her white sweater, making her catch her breath. A glowing log dropped in the grate, momentarily rousing Lobo who growled and then subsided. She heard the sounds, but they seemed remote. They had nothing to do with her and Weylin.

Nothing mattered but Weylin and his caresses. He slid her sweater over her head and unhooked her bra. He tasted her breasts, teeth nipping at her nipples until she moaned in pleasurable need, arching against him.

She wanted to be closer to him, had to be closer. She burned to consume him, to be consumed. She held his head to her breasts, intoxicated by his caresses, by his beguiling male scent.

"Weylin," she murmured. "Oh, Weylin..."

He lifted his head to look at her, and through her half-closed eyes she saw his face, unguarded, yearning.

"Beautiful," he whispered. "Jenna, you're so beautiful."

He crushed her against him, his lips hard on hers, the velvet rasp of his tongue inside her mouth more potent than any brandy. She wanted him never to stop kissing her; she yearned to experience the full range of the passion building between them. Her fingers crept under his shirt to stroke the warm, smooth skin of his back. He growled, deep in his throat, running his hands down to cup her buttocks.

Suddenly she was sliding, he was sliding, and they both slipped off the settee onto the braided rug, landing half on top of Lobo who, with a yelp, freed himself and retreated behind the settee.

As Jenna tried to untangle herself from Weylin she began to laugh and, after a moment, he joined in. They held each other and laughed and laughed until he stopped to nuzzle her throat and her own laughter trailed away.

The coals of the fire glowed warmly, and the blinking lights from the tree in the corner cast shifting colored shadows onto the walls and ceiling. As Jenna gazed dreamily at the only unblinking light, a white star at the tip of the pine, her hands lazily caressed Weylin's nape.

Their shared laughter hadn't lessened her desire but had subtly altered how she felt. There was no need to hurry; they had forever. The wonderful glowing warmth that bound them to each other was as bright and steady as the white star and would never diminish, would always last. It was theirs to share.

Weylin's lips started a slow, delicious journey from her throat toward her lips, and Jenna sighed in anticipation, closing her eyes. The image of the star, now red, remained behind her closed lids.

Red star. Pentacle. Pentagram. A magic symbol to ward off evil. Something else too, on the edge of her mind. Let it go; it didn't matter—only Weylin mattered. Only being in his arms.

His lips joined hers. As she began to ease into the turbulent current of passion, Jenna remembered. Pentagram in the palm. The werewolf. If, while in the form of a man, he sees a pentagram in the hand of a woman, he knows she's destined to be his victim when he changes into his more sinister form, into a wolf.

Victim?

The word sent a chill through Jenna, making her pull free. She edged away from Weylin and crossed her arms over her bared breasts.

Not that she believed in werewolves—it wasn't that at all—but he'd traced the five-pointed star in her palm. He thought of her as a victim. His victim. Not to stalk and to ravage, beastlike. No, he was definitely all man, and he'd as good as told her she was his to use as he pleased. Not a sharing—it would be a taking. Predator and victim.

Instead of anger, a deep sadness arose in Jenna and brought tears to her eyes. He could never be the man she'd willingly give her heart to, despite the wild magic that drew them together. She couldn't allow herself to be beguiled by his hypnotic allure. It wasn't love. She didn't love him; she wouldn't love him. They were poles apart. California and Alaska. The bright hot sun of Santa Anas and the dim cold sun of Arctic winters.

When he reached for her she got to her feet, retrieving her sweater and bra from the settee and holding them awkwardly in front of her.

Weylin stood up. "Jenna?" Bewilderment lined his brow, an incipient anger sparked in his green eyes.

"It's no use. Nothing can work between us." She blinked away the tears. "I should never have come to Julian."

"If it's those damn dogs—"

"This has nothing to do with the dogs! It has to do with you and with me. I told you before I'm not a conquest. That's all you want, and so I made up my mind when I first said it never to see you again. I'm sorry I didn't hold to that, but—"

She couldn't go on. He knew as well as she did how his touch excited her, that being near to him was the most potent stimulant in existence.

She was withdrawing now cold turkey. It was the only way to deal with Weylin Matthews.

"I wish—" she began before her voice wobbled and her throat closed with grief. Again she fought tears. What did she wish for? A different Weylin? A different Jenna? Because nothing else could close the gap separating them. "Good night," she managed to choke out as she turned toward the stairs.

She half expected to feel his hand on her shoulder, to be whirled, protesting, into his arms, and she held herself tense as she walked past the Christmas tree, the shining white star blurred by her tears.

He didn't come after her.

In her room, she heard the muted roar of the Mercedes and looked out the window in time to see the red eyes of its taillights receding into the darkness.

Where was he going?

I don't care, she told herself. From now on whatever Weylin does has nothing to do with me. She bit back a sob.

From downstairs came a long, quavering howl. Lobo sounded exactly the way she felt, and Jenna burst into fresh sobs. After a few minutes she remembered that Sam kept the wolf in a utility room off the kitchen at night, where there was a pet door that opened into a fenced run. In his rush away from the house, Weylin might have forgotten to put Lobo to bed.

Jenna wiped away her tears, pulled on her sweater, and opened the door. She heard the scuff of Lobo's claws on the floor below and sighed. She'd better go down and put the wolf where he belonged.

By the blinking lights of the Christmas tree, she shut Lobo into the utility room. Stopping by the tree on her way back upstairs, she wondered whether she should turn off the lights. There was no telling when Weylin would return, and with a live tree it wasn't wise to leave the lights on all night. She reached for the plug.

"Leave them on, Jenna," Sam's voice said from behind her.

Startled, she whirled. He stood in the doorway wearing a robe over pajamas.

"I—I didn't hear you come downstairs," she stammered.

"I heard the car drive off, and then old Lobo complained, so I came to put him to bed. I see you did it for me."

"I—yes." Jenna cleared her throat, thankful the room wasn't better lit. She didn't want Sam to get a good look at her tear-reddened eyes, even though he must know something was wrong by the way Weylin had roared away.

"Come and sit for a few minutes," Sam suggested.

Jenna hesitated. She could say she was tired. Yet she didn't especially want to go up to the room with the yellow roses and be alone with her thoughts.

"I want to talk to you," Sam added.

Slowly Jenna crossed to where he stood on the hearth and sat down on a straight-backed chair of polished pine.

Sam eased himself into the recliner opposite her. "I guess part of the trouble is that Weylin didn't have a happy childhood," he said. "My son, his father, set the boy a bad example. Emery just wasn't much good and that's a fact. He was our only child and sickly as a baby. I guess we spoiled him, his ma and me."

An ember crackled, and sparks flew up the chimney of the fireplace. The tree lights blinked on and off, coloring Sam's white mustache sometimes red, sometimes green.

"Emery was lazy," Sam went on baldly. "He thought the world owed him, and darned if the world didn't seem to agree. His first wife was the only daughter of Jarvis Whittaker, a self-made millionaire. Jarvis took Emery into his company, Whittaker Enterprises, making him a figurehead vice-president. Soon after, Jarvis and his daughter were in a bad car accident. Killed her outright and smashed Jarvis up pretty bad. He was in a coma for months and then very slowly got better, but he never was himself again. He had good men running things, so Whittaker Enterprises, and his other holdings too, had no problems.

"In the meantime, Emery married Ruth, an English gal who never had the guts to say boo to a goose. She had Weylin right off. The marriage was a mistake. Emery was always one for the women, and Ruth couldn't handle him. Weylin grew up without anyone paying him much mind."

"Something he said made me think he was pretty lonely as a boy," Jenna murmured.

Sam nodded. "Even when he was a tad he was a smart one though. Always knew what was going on, yet he never let anyone know how he felt. I didn't have as much time for him as I should have, 'cause Ma was pretty sick those years before she died.

"Anyway, old Jarvis was never right after the accident, and he made the mistake of giving Emery, who'd inherited the daughter's shares in the company, power of attorney as far as Whittaker Enterprises was concerned. I think, young as he was, even Weylin knew that was the same as turning a bear loose in a pantry. Emery spent his time drinking and gambling and running around on the company's money, never paying any mind to what needed doing. Ruth left him, and he was close to milking the company dry when he fell overboard from a friend's yacht and drowned."

Sam leaned forward. "Now all those years Emery was taking from the business and not putting back,

Weylin watched him. As soon as he finished at USC,
Weylin went into the company and tried to salvage
what he could. As long as his father lived though,
there wasn't much the boy could do. You see what I'm
leading up to?"

"I'm not quite sure."

"It'll come clear. Emery died and Weylin got old
Jarvis Whittaker, who was in his eighties by then, to
transfer the power of attorney to him. That was five
years back, and the boy's turned the company around.
They're making money hand over fist. At first I was
all for it; then I realized he'd made the dang business
his life. I'm disappointed in Weylin; I have to say it.
All the boy can think about is money. He's tried too
hard to be different from his father, and he's gone
astray from what counts."

"He does seem to be awfully competitive," Jenna
noted, Sam's forthrightness bringing out equal can-
dor in her. "It seems like he always has to win."

"That's Weylin." Sam shook his head. "Wish I
knew how to undo that fixation, but the truth is I
don't." He looked at Jenna. "Trouble is, he's got
himself so much knowhow that he hasn't lost at anything in years."

Jenna took a deep breath. "Sam, I hate to ask, but
could you drive me into San Diego now so I can catch
a flight? I have to get back to Anchorage as soon as I
can, or else—" She bit her lip. "I have to go home,"
she finished.

"I'll take you." He got up and reached a hand to
Jenna, helping her to her feet, but continuing to hold
her hand for a moment. "You must know all about
alpha males, gal; you know they can be tough ones to

handle. Go home and think things over. Just don't give up on him completely, that's all I ask.''

Tears filled Jenna's eyes. ''Where Weylin's concerned, I can't promise anything, Sam. Not one single thing.''

Six

Alaska seemed impossibly dark and cold when Jenna deplaned at Anchorage International on Christmas Day. The sky was overcast; there was no glimmer of sun, and the weather report predicted three to four inches of snow.

At least the snow will be good for mushing, she told herself. That's what she intended to do—spend every minute she could on the trail with the dogs. She'd do her best to train them for the Iditarod, so that even though she stood no chance of running the race with them, at least they might be able to qualify with another musher. Weylin hadn't yet sold the dogs. She'd work with them until he did.

They were a good team, with the potential to be a great one. If she had the time she'd see they reached their potential. How could she ever explain to Weylin how rewarding it was to take fourteen dogs and pull them together into a team? How could she make him understand that she tried to train the animals so they'd enjoy the process, enjoy sledding, enjoy racing? Few things were more exciting than riding the runners behind a team of well-trained huskies who were having the time of their lives pulling a sled.

No, Weylin would never understand. She'd been right to leave California when she had, right to leave him. She had nothing in common with a man who didn't appreciate dog sledding—who thought winning was more important than enjoying.

If she'd been right though, why did she feel so down?

She was tired, that's what it was. A good night's sleep would do wonders.

By New Year's Day, Jenna had to admit to herself that Weylin wasn't easy to dismiss from her mind. She couldn't stop thinking about him. She kept remembering everything they'd done together, the touch of his hand, the exciting warmth of his embrace. You'll never see him again, she admonished herself. Get on with your life. Forget him.

But she'd notice a lean, lithe man striding purposefully ahead of her and her pulses would pound. She'd be certain he was Weylin until he turned and she would see an unfamiliar profile. Or the phone would ring and her breath would catch before she picked it up. The call was never from Weylin, of course. Why did she imagine it might be?

She learned the meaning of heartache. Nothing else described the heaviness in her chest, the pang of loneliness because no other man was like Weylin, would ever be like Weylin.

With the dogs though, she could forget him for a while. The only problem was Chingo. Daily he seemed to grow more obstinate and perverse.

"Yeah, I had some trouble with him," Joe said when she asked. "I thought it was because he wasn't used to me, but he's one tough number. Chingo's determined to show who's boss, and it's not going to be his musher. Maybe a couple of licks with the whip would straighten him out."

"I don't use a whip on the dogs; you know that."

Joe shrugged. "Some do, and it doesn't seem to mess them up."

"It's not my way. In the first place I don't like to whip an animal, and in the second place punishment does no good unless it immediately follows the wrongdoing. I think it demoralizes the other dogs to see one of the team being whipped in front of them. No, I'll have to think of another way to bring Chingo into line."

A week later, after a night's camp-out, she was ten miles northeast of Anchorage at noon, with the sun barely above the trees. The dogs were running well through a couple of inches of new-fallen snow covering the packed trail. Hoarfrost covered every tree with sparkling white and the Chugach Mountains pierced a deep blue sky, a sight so beautiful her breath caught with wonder.

Riding the sled runners, she looked over her team with pride. The huskies were gorgeous dogs, with their masked faces and bushy tails curled high over their rumps. A few were blue-eyed; most were dark-eyed. Their ears were pricked to catch every sound.

A good-looking team, and Chingo, for once, was tending to business, leading the team at a steady trot.

The snow squeaked under the sled runners in the zero temperature.

"Haw," she called to Chingo, giving him the command to turn left, for the trail wound through a spruce grove before curving back toward the city.

Chingo obeyed and swung to the left, the other dogs following. She banked the sled for the turn, then almost fell off the runners when, with a snarling bark, Chingo abruptly picked up speed before the sled was straight again. The entire team began to run full out behind him, and Jenna's eyes widened when she saw the reason.

A bull moose stood in the trail ahead, hindquarters to them, antlered head swung around to stare at them. Would the moose contest the trail or amble off? Jenna tensed. No good to call "Gee" or "Haw," to head the dogs right or left, and then have the moose choose the same direction. She pulled out her jangler made of bells and bottle caps and shook it, the bells adding to the dogs' clamor, hoping the moose would bolt one way or the other before she had to make a decision.

The moose stepped off the trail to the right. To Jenna's annoyed consternation, Chingo started after him, team and sled following, slowing in the deeper, unpacked snow.

"Whoa, Chingo, whoa!" Jenna shouted, stomping on the brake and grabbing for the snow hook, a sharp piece of curved metal attached to the sled by a line.

Chingo paid not the least attention, still pulling after the moose despite the brake. Before Jenna could throw out the hook to anchor the sled, he managed to lead the team between some birch saplings and tangle the harnesses, bringing all the dogs to a halt. Jenna jumped off the sled, holding it back so it didn't hit the wheel dogs. She stomped the hook into the snow.

The dogs struggled to free themselves, most yapping frenziedly, still keyed to chasing the moose.

"Down," she called.

Some obeyed. Others, it seemed to her, looked to see what Chingo was doing. He was chewing on his harness! Definitely a no-no, especially for a lead dog.

"You!" she yelled, advancing on him. She'd never been so furious with a dog.

"Having a little trouble?" The mocking voice came from somewhere behind her.

Weylin!

Jenna spun around so fast she tripped on a half-hidden log and sprawled in the snow. She scrambled to her feet, so shocked at his sudden appearance she couldn't even think, much less speak. Brushing angrily at the snow clinging to her face, she glared at him.

What was he doing there?

He snowshoed past her to the dogs. Chingo eyed him a moment, then resumed chewing the harness.

"Shape up, Chingo," Weylin snapped. He reached out and rapped the lead dog's nose with the side of his mittened hand.

Chingo backed away as far as the tangled harness would let him, eyes fixed on Weylin.

"Let's get some order into this mess," Weylin said, turning his back on Chingo to look at her. "What do we do first?"

With Weylin's help, it was simple enough to untangle harness and dogs, and then straighten out the team and the sled.

"Now what?" he asked.

"They have to pull the sled back onto the trail again." She stared at him. "How did you come to be here, anyway?"

"Joe told me you'd camped out here and the trail you'd take back to town. I was waiting for you to come along when this big damn moose roared by and almost trampled me underfoot. Then I heard the dogs set up a clamor and followed the noise."

That hardly explained what he was doing there. All she could think of was that he'd sold the dogs and had come to find them. Anger began to simmer inside her. She didn't want him anywhere near her.

Turning to the team, she called, "Line out," the signal for the dogs to stretch the gang lines taut and get ready to pull.

Chingo turned and looked at her as if to say, "What for?" If ever a dog looked insolent, this one did. Jenna muttered under her breath. Of all the times for Chingo to act up, he'd picked the worst.

Before she could decide how to discipline the leader, Weylin joined her.

"Chingo," he said firmly, "line out!"

Chingo slowly faced front and pulled the lines taut, the other dogs following suit behind him. Weylin glanced at her.

Jenna bit her lip. Damn that dog. Why would he obey Weylin and not her? Hadn't she trained him in the first place? Hadn't she lavished time and attention on him? Made him the lead dog?

"Maybe you'd better lend me your snowshoes and ride the sled runners in my place," she told Weylin frostily.

"Hey, I don't even know the commands," he protested. "Don't be upset. You can't help it if Chingo would sooner obey a man than a woman."

She shook her head, knowing that wasn't it; Joe had had trouble with Chingo too. She'd always believed certain dogs had a sense of humor; maybe this was Chingo's idea of a joke.

"Look," Weylin went on, "you explained to me about alpha males. Chingo's one. So maybe he has to have an alpha male in charge."

"Alpha dogs usually prefer female mushers." Her tone was icy. So Weylin called himself an alpha, did he?

"Chingo's the exception, then. You saw how he snapped to when I gave the order."

"Are you saying you can do better with Chingo than I can?"

He shrugged. "If I knew the right commands."

She smiled, a mere baring of her teeth. "I'll teach them to you; there are only a few."

Weylin glanced from her to the dogs and back. "Deal."

"'Hike' means go, 'whoa' means stop, 'gee' for right, 'haw' for left, 'come gee' for a right U-turn, 'come haw' for a left U-turn. Got those?"

"'Hike' for go? Sounds like football. Shouldn't it be 'mush'?"

"'*Marche*' was what the French *voyageurs* used to call to their dogs in the old days. It got corrupted to 'mush.' Practically no one uses the word today. Mushers sometimes say 'Get on,' or 'Let's go,' or 'Yakes.' These dogs are used to 'hike.'"

"Okay, 'hike' it is. And 'whoa,' 'gee' and 'haw.'"

"That's enough to get you back to town if you're lucky."

He raised his eyebrows. "You don't have much confidence in me, do you?" He held out his hand. "Here's the key to the snow machine I left by the road. You'll find it by following my tracks." Weylin bent to unfasten the snowshoes.

He was actually going to take her up on it. Try to mush a team of dogs into town from ten miles out, when he didn't know the trail and had never driven a team of dogs in his life. Of course, the dogs knew the trail, and they could get back. All right, let him find out how stubborn Chingo could be. If she had to, she could always rescue him before it got too dark. And she sincerely hoped he'd get his comeuppance in the meantime.

Weylin stepped onto the runners, and Jenna opened her mouth to tell him that because of the deeper snow off the trail he ought to help the dogs by pumping, pushing with one foot while the other stayed on the runners. No, she thought. Let him wonder why Chingo doesn't want to pull.

"Hike!" Weylin called.

Chingo threw himself into the harness, pulling for all he was worth and, naturally, the other dogs followed their leader. The sled creaked off through the spruce trees, heading for the trail. Just before it disappeared from sight, Weylin turned and waved to her.

She didn't wave back.

It's a fluke, she assured herself as she tromped back along Weylin's snowshoe trail. Sooner or later he'll run into trouble.

She found the snow machine, started it, and headed for town, using a trail near the road, since the machines weren't allowed on sled trails any more than the dogs were allowed on ski trails.

Already she'd begun to worry. Not about Weylin, but about the dogs. What if they chanced on another moose and chased it? What if Weylin got dumped from the sled and then the dogs hung the sled up far off the trail? He'd be all right, despite having to slog back without snowshoes, but how about the dogs?

She should have had more sense than to let a *cheechako* mush her team. Damn Weylin—he seemed to bring out the worst in her. Jenna throttled down the snow machine. She'd try to pace the sled, paralleling the dog sled trail as best she could so she'd be close by to help when something went wrong, as she was certain it would.

She worried all the way into town, despite several reassuring glimpses of the team with Weylin still riding the runners. By the time she'd parked the machine in Maki's lot on the north edge of town and hurried around to the dog yard at the back of the buildings, Weylin was approaching with the team.

How well they ran, Jenna thought, proud of her dogs. Even Chingo. She'd been foolish to fret; she'd trained the team so well they could even bring in a *cheechako* without any trouble.

"Whoa," Weylin called as the dogs trotted into the yard.

Chingo obeyed immediately, and the huskies stood in their harnesses, tongues lolling and tails wagging, none tired enough to lie down. What a great bunch they were.

Weylin hopped off the sled. "I'll help you unharness them if you'll show me the right way." He grinned. "Exhilarating as hell, riding those runners, and not nearly as hard as you mushers make it out to be. I'll bet I could enter that March race and win it myself. What's the big deal?"

She stared at him open-mouthed. Weylin? In the Iditarod? Ridiculous!

"Obviously you don't agree with me," he said.

"No, I certainly don't. You'd be lucky to come in at all, much less win. The Iditarod's not for *cheechakos*, green to mushing. It's a long, hard, cold trail."

"I've got two months to practice. In that length of time I can learn more than enough. Chingo's already my dog; he does everything I ask. He knows enough not to fool around with me."

She laughed. "Are you actually serious?"

Weylin's nod was curt.

Her eyes narrowed. "I don't think you can do it. In fact, I'll bet you can't. I don't believe you'll even make the money—that's the first twenty—much less win."

"I'll be first. Wait and see. And I'll take that bet. What's the prize?"

"Money. Winners split the purse on a percentage basis. First price can be $25,000 or more."

"No, I mean what're *you* betting?"

Jenna blinked. She hadn't thought. "Uh—five dollars?"

Weylin shook his head. "Not money. The winner of the bet gets to choose the penalty he wants from the loser. Fair enough?"

Jenna frowned at him, then relaxed. No matter what he decided on, she didn't have a chance in the world of losing this bet.

"Whatever he or *she* chooses," she said, amending his terms.

Weylin nodded, watching her. After a moment he said, "Let's make it more exciting. Except for Chingo, I'll let you keep on with the Maki dogs so you can enter the race too."

For a moment she couldn't believe her ears. She'd naturally thought he intended to race the Maki team.

"That ought to cut out this nonsense you've been handing me about not caring whether you come in first or not." He smiled one-sidedly. "You'll have to beat me to win. Can you say you don't want to beat me?"

"I'll be ahead of you, you can count on that."

"The only way you can come in ahead of me is to win the race. And you won't. I will. Chingo and I. We understand each other."

"You'll need more than Chingo." Her tone was caustic.

He waved a hand. "I'll hire a trainer to work with me, the best there is, and let him pick out the rest of my dog team."

Jenna bristled at the edge of mockery in his words. "A better trainer than I am—is that what you mean?"

"One who works better with Chingo, at least."

She drew herself up. "I'm an excellent trainer. This team's going to win the Iditarod. Without Chingo. To hell with Chingo—you can have him. I'll use Sonia; she's the alpha female of the pack, and she's got the ability to make a better leader than Chingo could ever be."

"Then why weren't you using her?"

Jenna glared at him. "She's his mate. As long as he was in the pack, she'd let him lead. That's the way Sonia is."

"She's my kind of woman."

"Obviously." She spat the word.

Weylin's green eyes held hers. "You ought to be satisfied now. You have your own team, and you'll be running the Iditarod. Everything you could ask for, isn't that right?"

"All I want from you, at any rate."

He put mittened hands on her shoulders. "Is it?"

For a moment she was almost caught in the net of enchantment he could weave with his eyes and his touch. She couldn't deny the thrill of response that flashed through her, but she forced herself to pull away.

"You heard what I said," she told him. "If you want help with your dogs, I'll be happy to do what I can. Otherwise—"

"Why do you think I came back to Anchorage, Jenna?"

She shrugged, nodding at the dogs.

"No, not because of the dogs. Or Maki Equipment. Why do you keep running away from me, Jenna?"

"I made a mistake in going to California, then compounded the mistake by staying." She turned to the dogs. "It's time we unharnessed and fed them. If you're going to be a musher, one of the first things you have to learn is how and what to feed your dogs. Like any form of transportation, they don't run without the right fuel." She crouched to unfasten Chingo.

"I'll do him," Weylin told her. "He's my dog. And you didn't answer my question."

"Because we don't fit together." She released Sonia from the harness next to Chingo and led the fawn-and-white female to her wooden house, chaining her there.

Weylin followed with Chingo. "To my way of thinking we fit wonderfully," he said.

She refused to look at him, afraid she'd see in his eyes what she knew neither of them had forgotten—the memory of Christmas Eve in Julian and their shared passion.

"I don't mean—" She broke off. No, she wasn't going to involve herself with him in that way again. She didn't even want to discuss anything that had been between them. "Make sure Chingo's chain is fast," she finished.

"Why do we have to chain the dogs anyway? There's a fence around their yard; they can't run off."

"If huskies aren't chained so they can't get at each other, they fight. Males with males, females with females. Dogs can be maimed, even killed."

"These dogs? They seemed so happy pulling the sled, and they work so well as a team."

"That's because they're in harness and the musher is boss. Left alone and unchained—" She shook her head.

"But you said Chingo was the alpha male and the others knew it. Would they fight him?"

"They'd gang up on him, most likely. The males, anyway. Huskies are what they are. You have to allow for it and take precautions. They'd never hurt a human they knew, not deliberately. A stranger might be a different story."

"I see I still have a few details to learn."

"Yes, you do. More than a few. I've worked with dogs since I was a kid, and they still surprise me sometimes."

"As I once told you, I'm a quick learner."

She measured him with her gaze. "In some ways."

"How am I supposed to take that."

"For one thing, you still haven't learned that winning isn't everything."

"In my experience it has been. Losers get nowhere."

"What about love?" she demanded. "How can you win or lose? If you love someone, you love him, that's all."

"And if she doesn't love you in return, you lose." His smile was wary. "You can't deny that."

"You don't understand. Love's not a contest. Or a conquest either. Love just *is*."

"Maybe we're talking about two different things," he said.

"We have been ever since we met," she told him, swallowing hard at the lump in her throat.

Seven

———

A quiet mind. Jenna nodded as she pulled on her boots over two pairs of socks. If she expected to keep the confidence of her team now that she'd switched Sonia to lead dog, she had to be quietly confident herself.

"Things happen at the right time to those who have quiet minds," an Eskimo musher had told her when, during her first year in Alaska, he stopped to help her untangle dogs and harnesses. "Sila dislikes angry minds, and the dogs are part of Sila. We all are."

Sila, she'd learned later, was the Eskimo word for the spirit of the universe, which included the thoughts of man and beast.

Having a quiet mind wasn't easy for her since Weylin had decided to enter the Iditarod. Her determination to prove to him she could beat him took a lot of fun out of the training. Besides, she never knew when she might encounter Weylin in the dog yard or on the trails around Anchorage. So far she hadn't met him, but she'd heard he was running with his new team headed by Chingo. She'd also heard he'd hired one of the top mushers, a triple champion, to train both him and the dogs.

Jenna didn't believe Weylin could learn enough in two months to be a real threat. On the other hand, he'd probably wind up with a first-rate team, and it was the dogs who won races, after all. It wouldn't do to underestimate the team, even if she was sure he didn't stand a chance.

If ever there was someone with an unquiet mind, Weylin was that person. She mustn't let him unsettle hers. Which was simple to decide but tricky to put into practice. Especially when her every other thought seemed to be about him.

Enough of Weylin. Jenna pulled on her red parka with its hood ruff of wolverine fur and picked up gloves, mitts, and car keys. She'd loaded the car the night before except for one last pack of food, and she had enough gear for the seventy-five-mile run she planned to make in the next two days.

As she drove toward the dog yard near Maki Equipment, where both her team and Weylin's were lodged, she reflected that for a man who'd objected to keeping one team of dogs because it was a frill, he'd certainly gone overboard. Instead of fourteen there were now twenty-six huskies of various types to feed and care for. He'd had to buy new equipment and hire a full-time handler.

All because he couldn't resist a challenge. Because of his driving need to win.

The dogs set up a clamor when she came into the yard. Jenna greeted her thirteen one at a time, pausing long enough to pat them each quickly before she went to the storage shed. Before she pulled out her own seven-foot sled of ash, she stopped a moment to eye Weylin's. He'd bought one of the new-type toboggan-sleds. Instead of the basket—the body of the sled—being held several inches above the runners by eight or so wooden stanchions, it sat on a sheet of plastic extending the length of the sled directly on top of the runners.

Some mushers swore the new sleds with their lower centers of gravity were more stable, and the innovation did eliminate the breakable stanchions. Jenna, though, preferred her traditional design, time-tested through hundreds of years of dog sledding.

As she pulled her sled into the yard, she admired its lines, the limber curves of the brush bow at the front of her basket, the higher drive bow—her handlebar—in back. Pleasing to the eyes and entirely functional.

The dogs, seeing the sled, renewed their clamor, eager to run.

"A working dog is a happy dog," her veterinarian uncle had often told her. "Lying around inside houses makes neurotic animals out of dogs bred for a purpose: hunting, pulling carts or sleds, herding, guarding. Give a dog something to do and you make him happy."

Jenna set the snow hook firmly, then laid the harnesses and lines on the snow in front of the sled. She hurried to unchain the first dog to be hooked up. Sonia would be last. When she walked Sonia on a leash along the line of hitched dogs before hooking her, it seemed to inspire the team to behave.

Once all the dogs were in harness, Jenna stood for a moment at the head of the team. Sonia, ears pricked, watched her face carefully, waiting for a command. Like the other huskies, Sonia seemed to be smiling, the husky's normal expression unless upset. Jenna grinned back at them, then strode back to remove the snow hook from the ground and stow it in the sled. She climbed on the runners.

"Line out," she called. Then, "Hike!"

Sonia led the team through the gate at a trot and, following Jenna's orders to turn left or right, soon had them heading east, paralleling Glenn Highway. To the north, across the ice-floe-choked water of Knik Arm, the snow-covered Alaska Range thrust into the dark blue morning sky. Mount McKinley, though, was hidden by its own clouds. It wasn't quite ten, so the sun hadn't risen, but the day promised to be fair. With the thermometer hovering around zero and little wind, it was perfect sledding weather, the kind of day dogs and mushers alike enjoyed.

Jenna intended to follow the local trails near the Chugach Mountains for an hour or so before heading into Chugach State Park. The dogs were accustomed to twenty-mile jaunts; she meant to lengthen their time on the trail so that by March both she and they could easily make fifty miles or more at a stretch.

Weylin didn't have his team out yet, so there'd be little chance of running into him. That's the way she wanted it. Jenna took a deep breath of the crisp January air, feeling each nostril stick together inside briefly, a sign it was zero or below. After the Iditarod, Weylin would leave Alaska and she'd never have to worry about seeing him again. Until then, she'd do her best to dislodge him from her mind.

And from her heart? She pressed her lips together in denial. He'd never had a place in her heart; he didn't have one now—would never have. Her heartache was due to injured pride and hurt feelings, nothing else. After the Iditarod in March she'd have a quiet mind and a whole heart. Until then...

Stop thinking about the man, she warned herself. He isn't your entire life. How can he be? You didn't even know he existed before November. You lived happily for twenty-three years without Weylin Matthews; you can certainly live the rest of your life the same way. Be happy without him.

Had he ever been really happy? After listening to his grandfather, Jenna could see how Weylin's lonely childhood might have scarred him. She felt a pang of sympathy for the young boy who'd tried to change into a wolf to run away from unhappiness.

She wondered if the book of magic formulas he'd used had an incantation to support the Eskimo belief that a wolf could change into a killer whale and vice versa. A man would need a triple shape change for that—human to wolf to killer whale. What would the requirements be? A whaleskin belt? Too bad if the whale change took place and you weren't near water....

Jenna shook her head. What nonsense she had let herself drift into. Why, she'd been a completely practical person before Weylin entered her life. Knew exactly what she intended to do next. Followed a logical course. Controlled her life. She'd planned ahead for the day she'd meet a man she could love, a man who'd love her in return. She knew exactly what he'd be like.

First, he'd love dogs. Love Alaska and the outdoors. He'd understand the joy of the trail. While he might like matching his talents against those of others, he wouldn't be so competitive that winning was everything to him, and he'd realize money wasn't all-important. He'd believe in commitment, even in marriage.

In short, he'd be a lot like she was.

He wasn't Weylin, not by any stretch of the imagination. Weylin was—well, he was impossible, no question of that. He wasn't for her.

If only she could forget how it felt to be in his arms, forget the warmth and smoothness of his skin under her fingers. If only she didn't long for the touch of his hand on her breast, the breathless excitement of his kiss. Just remembering kindled an expectant warmth deep within her.

For a moment she regretted she hadn't let herself be shaped and changed by the passionate magic they'd conjured up together in Julian. If they'd made love then instead of quarreling...

Stop, damn it, Jenna admonished herself. Do you or do you not want to do well in the Iditarod? Then keep your mind on the dogs and on the trail.

Just after two o'clock, Jenna stopped to feed the dogs a snack of cheese and tallow before she ate a few mouthfuls of trail mix washed down with some ice-cold coffee from her super-insulated thermos. Nothing stayed hot in this weather. When she started up again, she was well into Chugach Park, running through spruce and hemlock.

When she saw moose tracks on the trail she slowed the dogs, hoping to avoid having one or more of them step into the holes made by a moose breaking through the crust of snow. A misstep like that could badly lame a dog, even break its leg. She certainly didn't want any of her huskies injured in any way.

"Easy, Sonia," she called. "Easy, girl."

They left the tracks behind and Jenna encouraged the team into a trot again. "Gee," she called, seeing the loop to the right ahead, making ready to bank the sled into the turn.

Sonia swung to the right, followed by the other dogs. Because of the trees on either side, only when the sled came into the turn could Jenna see the trail ahead. To her consternation, another team was racing toward her.

"Whoa!" Jenna cried, hearing her call echoed by the other musher.

It was too late.

Her huskies tried to stop and managed to slow their pace, but finally were forced to attempt dodging the oncoming dogs. In a few seconds the two teams were hopelessly entangled. Dogs snarled, whined, and yipped, challenging one another while they struggled to free themselves. Jenna, who'd set her sled brake, leaped off the runners to avoid being thrown to the ground.

"You!" she gasped, staring at the man near the other sled.

"So what the hell do we do now?" Weylin demanded.

"Grab your whip and wade in," she told him. "We've got to separate the dogs before they get down to serious fighting."

As he reached for his whip he said, "I thought you never hit a dog."

"Use the butt if you have to—it beats getting chewed up. Once these huskies get to snapping they lose track of who's who. The combination of dog and wolf makes for a touchy animal.''

Jenna dragged her dogs one after another to the stake chain she hastily attached to two trees off the trail, hooking them on despite their continuing eagerness to mix it up with Weylin's team. Once her dogs were out of the tangle, she set up Weylin's hitch so he could do the same.

When all the dogs were safely chained, she took stock. Despite her carefulness, a husky's teeth had ripped one of her mitts and her down overalls were torn.

And she was mad as hell. Weylin had been roaring along the trail as though he was racing his team in the Rondy. Going far too fast for a turn, he'd have upset the sled, green musher that he was. Hadn't he learned anything? Jenna took a deep breath, preparing to let fly.

Weylin grinned one-sidedly, shaking his head. ''An L.A. freeway fender-bender traffic jam has nothing on a bunch of huskies all trying to claim the trail at the same time and place.''

Despite her anger she felt a flash of amusement at the comparison.

''And you're the feisty gal in the red Toyota who's about to tell off the guy in the Mercedes for going too fast,'' Weylin went on.

''Well, you were!''

''I got carried away. The dogs were so eager to run...'' He shrugged.

''Neither of us used our janglers before the turn to warn an oncoming sled, so I'm partly to blame. But—'' A mournful howl interrupted her, and she swung around to look at the dogs.

By chance, Chingo had been tethered at the end of Weylin's hitch nearest Sonia at the end of Jenna's. The two huskies gazed at each other, Sonia lifting her muzzle to answer Chingo's protest at their separation. Jenna couldn't help smiling.

"Star-crossed lovers," Weylin said, chuckling.

All Jenna's anger dissolved in laughter. She laughed so hard she choked and gasped, finally leaning against a spruce trunk for support. When she could focus she saw Weylin was in similar shape, hanging onto the bar of his sled.

What was so funny about the dogs, anyway? She couldn't understand it, but just looking at them threatened to set her off again. It was all so silly.

"Should we camp and look over the dogs?" Weylin asked, amusement still in his voice.

She stared at him, suddenly completely sober, words of refusal springing to her tongue. Camp? She had miles yet to travel that day—except that he was right about the dogs. She was almost sure there'd been no serious injuries, but she ought to treat any bites and make certain none of her dogs were lame before she went on. That might take an hour or more, and then there would be the time spent reharnessing the dogs afterward.

"There's a small clearing." Weylin pointed into the spruces. "About the right size for two teams to camp."

It might be wise to camp before she assessed the dogs' conditions. If any of them had strained a muscle or pulled a tendon in the mix-up, they'd have a chance to rest for a few hours. And she wanted to run them at night anyway. Camp now, examine the huskies, eat, sleep a few hours, then hit the trail.

But camp with Weylin? Jenna fought to ignore the thrill of expectation tingling along her spine.

"No need to camp together," she said brusquely.

"I'd hoped to pick up a few pearls of wisdom about sleeping outdoors in this winter wonderland." His tone was regretful. "I've never been much of a camper."

Jenna wavered despite her suspicion of irony in his use of "winter wonderland." She couldn't believe Weylin had so quickly changed his mind about the Alaskan cold. Still, the day *was* gorgeous, sky and snow reddening with the setting sun, and the air was brisk and clean. The stand of spruce protected them from the light breeze, and the trees around them gave her a cozy, homelike feeling. How could he be immune to the beauty and, yes, the wonder of the country?

And wouldn't she be neglectful if she didn't help him out? He'd hired a dog trainer, but how much had the man taught him about camping in the winter?

"I'll be happy to show you what I can about winter camps," she said at last, eyeing him warily. She didn't quite trust Weylin.

"Great. What do we do first?"

After he'd unpacked his sled, she checked his sleeping bag and nodded in approval—down, enclosed inside a specially designed outer bag plus a bivouac bag.

"Good choice," she said, "if a bit large."

Weylin gazed down at the bag. "I see what you mean. Big enough for two if they cuddled together."

Since that's exactly what she was thinking, Jenna flushed. She hoped her cheeks were red enough from the cold so he wouldn't notice. Ignore him, she told herself.

All very well to say, but how could she ignore the quick lash of desire in her loins when she pictured them together in his bag? His eyes held hers until she grew breathless.

"Caribou skin provides the best insulation, according to some of the mushers," Jenna said hastily. "The Eskimos use it. Your bivvy bag is fine though. And you can use spruce boughs underneath."

"Whatever you suggest. All I know is that I've never worn so many layers of clothing in my life and still been cold."

"You shouldn't feel especially chilly right now."

He smiled. "At the moment, I'm not." Because you're standing next to me, his eyes suggested. And you could make me warmer still....

Jenna forced her gaze from his and busied herself with her own gear. "Keep moving and you won't feel the cold," she advised briskly. "We have a lot to do before you'll have the chance to try out your sleeping bag. The dogs' food has to be thawed and snow melted and warmed before we can feed and water them. With luck we'll get to eat our own grub a couple of hours from now. You can get started by lighting your camp stove."

Later, crouched by his stove, stirring the contents of a large pot that sat on it, Weylin looked over at Jenna, who was similarly engaged with her own stove, and shook his head, grimacing with distaste. "Awful-smelling stuff. Not so great to look at either, but my trainer swears by it for the dogs. Half lamb and chicken fat, he told me; most of the rest is horse meat and beef mixed with a little rice. Plus vitamins, liver, and some concoction to speed digestion. Costs more than my own food."

"No fish? I always mix in a little fish. Salmon's the best."

"He claims salmon's in the balls of glop the dogs snack on. These must be the most overfed animals in the world."

"If you want your dogs to do their best, you have to keep them fat and sassy."

Weylin glanced at the tethered huskies. "They look pretty lean to me, considering all the feed they get twice a day, not to mention the trail snacks in between."

"Fat's a figurative word. A working dog is never really fat."

Weylin grunted. "If anyone had told me I'd spend an Alaskan winter in the snow cooking dog food at zero temperatures, I'd have been sure he was crazy."

"All mushers are a little bit nutty," Jenna informed him. "Welcome to the club."

"I can believe that."

"You're in by your own choice."

His eyes narrowed. "I wonder."

"No one's forcing you to compete in the Iditarod. That's the only reason you're learning dog sledding."

"I have the feeling you're mixed up in there somewhere."

Jenna widened her eyes. "Just what are you accusing me of?"

"Stubbornness. If you'd given up on those damn dogs when I first told you they had to be sold, I'd never have gotten into this." He gestured toward the huskies and waved his hand to include the sleeping gear, the stoves, the sleds, the snow, the surrounding trees, and the Chugach peaks beyond.

"If I recall correctly, you *asked* me to continue caring for the team until you were able to sell the dogs." Her voice rose indignantly. "Why blame me?"

"How else could I go on seeing you?" he said plaintively. "What did I care about dogs?"

"Well, you're certainly not in the race because of me. It's your own stubborn competitiveness that's put you here, so don't go looking for a scapegoat."

"You misunderstand. What I meant—"

"I have to feed my dogs." Jenna shut off her stove and got to her feet. "If you don't like what you're doing, then don't do it, that's my advice." She began dishing up dog food, her back to Weylin but half expecting him to go on arguing.

I won't pay attention, she assured herself. I won't be enticed by his something-between-us lure again. If there is, so what? It can lead nowhere except to grief.

But Weylin said nothing, busying himself with his dogs while she fed and watered hers. Over an hour later, pans cleaned with snow and stowed on the sled, Jenna poked among the packages of food she'd taken along for herself, trying to decide what she wanted. Somehow, she didn't feel hungry.

It didn't do to skip a meal on the trail though. Both humans and beasts needed fuel to survive the cold. Only a faint red-gold alpenglow resisted the long January night. Jenna stared up at the stars, which were exceptionally bright in the dark winter sky. How they glittered, almost seeming to be, as Robert W. Service said in one of his poems, "dancing heel and toe."

Her lips curved into a smile as she recalled the poem: *The Cremation of Sam McGee*, a tongue-in-cheek tale of a musher determined to fulfill his dead and frozen friend's last wish, a desire to be cremated so that he'd finally find warmth in the Alaskan winter.

Weylin ought to appreciate Tennessee Sam Mc-Gee's final request. Impulsively she turned to Weylin.

"'There are strange things done in the midnight sun...'" she began in her best declamatory tone.

His first look of puzzlement changed to one of amusement as she went on, stanza after stanza.

"'The northern lights have seen queer sights...'" she intoned as she swung into the final quatrain.

When she stopped, Weylin clapped his mittened hands. "Bravo. I don't think I can remember a single poem, even though I had a seventh-grade English teacher who was certain we had nothing better to do than memorize entire volumes of poetry." He looked over her head. "Speaking of northern lights..."

Jenna drew in her breath as she gazed upward. The last of the alpenglow had vanished. Green light arced across the dark sky, with luminous blue and yellow feathering out from the shifting bands in one of the most brilliant auroral displays she'd ever seen.

"The red—" Weylin pointed "—I've never seen them that color before. Look, the red's hanging in the sky like a curtain of light. It's so low I swear if I climbed a spruce I could touch it."

Jenna whistled through her teeth, a high piercing sound that startled a couple of the dogs. When their howls died away, she said, "I whistled to make the lights dance faster. Watch."

"Hey, you could be right. Who taught you that?"

"The Eskimo children believe it. And listen, you can hear the lights; you always can when they dip low."

A faint crackling broke the night's quiet. The red fringe of light pulsed and shimmered, coloring the snow on the peaks.

"Uh-oh," Jenna said, "watch out or the headballs will get you. They're luminous red sky spirits, and if they capture you, you've had it. They'll play ball with your head."

Weylin grinned. "Eskimo kids again?"

She nodded. "But you can almost believe the lights are alive on a night like this."

"Instead of charged particles from the sun colliding with the Earth's atmosphere?"

"Spoilsport."

"I thought it was time to impress you with my vast store of scientific knowledge."

She made a face at him. "I'll stick to my meager stock of Eskimo lore. It's more appropriate when the aurora shines. They say, 'What pleases the eye, pleases the heart.' Tonight the lights do just that."

"Not only the lights, if we're talking about *my* heart." Weylin moved closer as he spoke, the white frost of his breath meeting and mingling with hers.

His eyes held hers; their message was bright and luminous. I want to touch you, hold you, kiss you. I want you.

Jenna felt pierced through to her inner being, electrified by irresistible desire. She opened her arms to Weylin.

Eight

Weylin touched his lips to Jenna's. Her nose and her cheek were cold, but her mouth felt warm under his. Warm and responsive, triggering an urgent need to hold her close to him unhampered by four layers of clothes—eight, if she had on as many as he did.

He yearned to feel her bare skin against his. How well he remembered being in Julian, her fire-warmed flesh soft and yielding to his caresses. He had to have more of her, more and more and more. Would he ever have enough?

She was beautiful, she was funny, and she was the most stubborn woman he'd ever met. A stubborn alpha female.

The passion in her kiss and the fervent way she pressed against him betrayed her. She wanted him. As she'd wanted him in Julian. What had gone wrong then? Jenna was no tease; he must have said something that made her change her mind. For the life of him he couldn't recall what it might have been.

Kissing her was addictive; he never wanted to let her go. She tasted of herself, fresh and sweet, a heady, intoxicating flavor. How he'd craved it those long weeks since Julian.

He wanted her—oh God, how he wanted her.

Weylin's lips left hers to caress her cheeks, her eyelids, the tip of her nose.

"Did you really come back to Alaska because of me?" she whispered.

"I couldn't give you up." His voice was husky with desire. "Believe me, I tried."

She laughed, low, breathless. "I've been trying too."

His arms tightened around her as his lips covered hers again, his tongue probing until she opened to him and he penetrated the warm, sweet recess of her mouth. Her tongue flicked lightly, tentatively over his. A hot current electrified his blood.

"Jenna, Jenna," he groaned.

He thought she breathed his name, but his heart beat so rapidly all he could hear was his own pulse pounding in his ears. He knew how, under those layers of clothing, the soft curves of her breasts would be peaking provocatively with the desire that stirred her, and he ached to caress them again, to put his mouth to her nipples until she writhed against him in an agony of need, lost to everything but the wild wonder between them....

In the back of his mind was the thought of his sleeping bag. Was she thinking of it too? Getting the two of them into that bag and out of enough clothes to make love needed cooperation. It wasn't something he could coax her into.

He was through coaxing anyway. If she wanted him as much as he wanted her, they'd spend this luminous night together in the sleeping bag joined in passion as wild and spectacular as the aurora. With Jenna it would be like nothing he'd ever experienced before.

"Damn this cold and snow," he said hoarsely.

Her eyes opened and looked into his. He tried to read her expression and failed.

"It's just as well," she said softly. "This isn't good for either of us."

It could be better than good, he thought. You know it, Jenna. He remained silent. No persuasion. No coaxing. Come to me, his eyes urged. Bend to me, merge with me, make love with me.

She leaned back in his arms. "We haven't eaten. One of the prime rules of the trail is not to go without food."

Damn the rules and the trail. What he hungered for wasn't food.

"In this country it doesn't pay to ignore rules," she went on as though he'd spoken aloud. "We'd better—"

Despite himself his arms tightened around her, cutting off her words. "You're lying if you tell me you'd rather eat right now," he growled.

"Just the same, I'm going to eat." She spoke breathlessly. "I shouldn't have—"

His mouth crushed hers in a long and savage kiss before he released her so abruptly she staggered.

"Call me when dinner's served." His words crackled.

"Dinner will be an individual effort," she said tartly. "Feel free to ask for help if you need any." Turning her back, she stalked off toward her sled.

He watched her, hands clenched inside his mitts. He wanted to run after her, throw her over his shoulder, haul her to his sleeping bag, and thrust her inside. Rip off her clothes and take her whether she wanted to or not.

Weylin swallowed, took a deep breath, and let it out slowly, seeing a plume of white float upward toward the waxing moon just visible above the trees. What was he thinking of? My God, what had this woman reduced him to?

He strode toward his sled, glancing at the dogs as he passed them. Chingo was asleep, nose in curled tail, at the extreme reach of his chain as close to Sonia as he could get. She'd done the same but, of course, they'd been tethered too far apart to touch.

Poor damn beasts.

Wolves now—they were better off when it came to sex. The male, running in the snow, followed the chosen female, and she would prolong the chase only to sweeten the final consummation. Warm in their thick gray coats, running together under the moon and finding at the end a savage joy with each other.

"Never mind, Chingo," he said under his breath. "You and I are going to win this race. Win the Iditarod. After that, I promise you and Sonia can be together." He looked over his shoulder at Jenna and nodded. Yes, he'd win that damn race or kill himself trying. And Jenna? She didn't come with the prize money. All the same, he was certain winning would make a difference.

He hadn't had to prove himself to a woman since he was seventeen and his expertise with a back dive had been the charm that turned on the red-haired cheerleader who lived down the street. He'd spent three months perfecting that dive. Funny how he remembered practising better than he recalled the name of the girl.

Women. He could take them and leave them. Only once had he thought maybe he'd found someone different. She'd played hard to get in the beginning and that had fooled him, although it took him six months to figure it out. Jenna, though, wasn't playing.

Would she last longer than six months? She wasn't like the women he usually chose, and it puzzled him how he could have involved himself so deeply without once taking her to bed.

She was obsessed with dogs, with training them, with Alaska. There was more in life than training dogs, although since he'd taken up mushing he could understand the fascination of the trail, and he was growing almost as fond of Chingo as he was of Lobo. Anchorage wasn't bad either, a clean, lively city surrounded by spectacular mountains. But this damn cold wilderness?

And how could you understand a woman who didn't care whether she came in first or not in the Iditarod? Perhaps she did care a little, but it really didn't seem to matter much to her if she didn't win as long as she proved she could make the run from Anchorage to Nome. Proved herself as a dog trainer. Winning was everything—she didn't seem to grasp that. He smiled slightly. She meant to beat him, though.

Once he won her, once they were together, she'd likely be as stubborn as ever. Would she make herself

available to come sailing with him at short notice? To
fly to Mexico if he took the notion? Like as not she'd
be too busy with the dogs. That is, if he even got her
out of Alaska in the first place.

No, he didn't see how it could be a long-term thing
with Jenna; they weren't suited to each other, as she'd
pointed out. Often.

Unfortunately, that didn't change how he felt about
her right now. He was as much obsessed with her as
she was with dog training, obsessed with her to the
exclusion of any other woman. It had to be Jenna or
no one, at least until he'd won her. He finally had the
way to do that figured out—win the Iditarod.

Which he intended to do anyway.

It's an obsession, Jenna thought as she crouched
over her camp stove, where her dehydrated stew was
warming in thawed-snow water. The man's taken over
my entire life. I can't go anywhere without looking for
him, do anything without thinking about him. When
I'm actually with him I'm as malleable as wax and
melt just as easily.

That's not love.

She glanced to where Weylin was stirring a pot on
his stove, and her eyes traced the clean line of his profile—stubborn chin, aquiline nose, broad forehead.
Her tongue explored the small cut on the inside of her
lips that was the result of that last wild kiss.

He'd been angry. He still was.

In a way she understood the anger. At the same
time, she resented it. Hadn't she been as aroused as
he? Wasn't it just as difficult for her to stop?

Of course, she shouldn't have kissed him in the first
place. But when those green eyes of his glowed into
hers he was hard to resist. She wanted him in a way

she'd never expected to want a man other than the one she meant to marry—desperately. Damn near overwhelmingly. Even now she had to fight to keep herself away from him—from him and that oversized sleeping bag where they'd be cozy and warm and together. Where they could make love.

Except it wouldn't be love. He didn't love her; he'd never told her he did. At least he was honest in that way. And what she felt for him couldn't be love. It was more like a kind of madness she'd never dreamed herself capable of.

Under that wolf-trimmed parka and the clothes beneath, his body was lean and hard and strong. She'd felt it against hers and had never forgotten. She wanted him to hold her again with no clothes to interfere. Wanted, wanted. Wanted him right now.

Jenna shook her head. Madness. Giving up all your plans and expectations, giving up what you believe in, just to spend a night in his arms. Would it be worth all that? Even if you believed it would be, would you feel the same afterward?

She sighed. Since they were there together she could hardly huddle off at one end of the camp while he brooded at the other. That was childish. Besides, she was supposed to be teaching him survival skills. Get your act together, she ordered herself.

She picked up her mug of stew and headed for Weylin. He looked up, saw her coming, and grinned crookedly. Straightening up from the stove, he put his mittened hand on his chest and recited:

Even a man who is pure in heart
And says his prayers by night

May become a wolf when the wolfsbane
blooms
And the winter moon is bright.

Jenna blinked, then smiled. "I doubt your seventh-grade teacher picked that for you to memorize."

"It was in that old incantation book—supposed to be an ancient Gypsy werewolf rhyme. I substituted winter for autumn to make it more appropriate. And you must be wearing wolfsbane perfume."

Who else but Weylin would come up with such a fantastically oblique apology?

"What is wolfsbane, anyway?" she asked.

"Aconite. A yellow-flowered poisonous plant."

"If you'll guarantee to keep it out of my stew, we can eat together. What're you cooking?" She peered into the pot. "Ugh, looks terrible."

"I was beginning to think so too. I might have done something wrong."

"For one thing, you've burned it. For another, you didn't add liquid." She shook her head as she turned off his stove. Thrusting her mug of stew at him, she said, "Eat this. I made double portions, and I'll get myself another serving. Don't you ever cook for yourself in California?"

"Not often."

"Well, you'll have to learn to feed yourself on the trail. If you don't—"

"I know—Alaska will get even with me. She has no use for *cheechakos*."

"It's true. You have to learn everything you can and learn it well. You and the dogs are by yourselves on the Iditarod run. For mile after mile there are no villages, not even trappers' cabins. Just winter wilderness."

"I won't take chances."

"Good, because you won't live to get a second one." I sound so preachy, Jenna thought. But how else can I impress Weylin with the dangers he'll be facing, the risks he'll be taking?

"Don't look so worried. I plan to stay alive. And well. We'll celebrate in Nome after I come in first." He grinned at her. "No matter how long I have to wait around for your team to arrive."

He really believes he's going to win, she marveled, refusing to rise to the bait. He can't visualize losing at anything.

Later, the meal over and their gear stowed away, they crawled into their separate sleeping bags, arranged side by side under a spruce-bough lean-to with a small fire burning outside at their feet.

Looking past the leaping flames, Jenna could see the shifting colors of the northern lights, paled by the immediate brightness of the fire. Beside her Weylin breathed evenly and slowly, and she wondered if he'd fallen asleep.

They'd shared the beauty of the night, shared laughter as well as anger. Perhaps this would be the last time the two of them would ever share anything again.

He might get to Nome, though she doubted he'd manage to finish the race. The annals of the Iditarod were filled with names of mushers who'd dropped out along the way. It wasn't like jogging along a California beach. Weylin would soon find out he'd bitten off more than he could chew.

After the race, what little they had in common now would vanish like snow in a warm chinook wind. Weylin would scrape the frost of Alaska from his

boots and go thankfully back to sunny California.
Probably he'd never visit Alaska again. One of his
Whittaker employees would be sent to handle Maki
Equipment in the future.

Thank heaven she hadn't completely given way to
the devastating surge of desire that had flung her into
his arms again. If she had, this sleeping bag would lie
empty while she snuggled next to him in his. Jenna
squeezed her eyes shut. No, she wouldn't look at him,
wouldn't let herself imagine what it would be like to be
with him. Whether or not they made love this night
wouldn't change a thing for Weylin, while for her...

She sighed. Of all the cities in all the states of this
country, she asked herself plaintively, why did he have
to come to mine?

The temperature hovered near twenty degrees—
normal for early March—as Jenna hooked up her huskies outside Mulcahy Stadium in Anchorage, where
the official starting line for the Iditarod was located.
Her team yipped and howled along with the other
eight hundred or so dogs waiting to begin the great
race.

She hadn't seen Weylin since that January camp
they'd shared, though she'd heard from Joe that
Weylin's dog trainer swore his was one of the best
teams he'd ever put together and Chingo was a real
winner. Weylin, the trainer told Joe, was "born to be
a musher."

She hadn't seen Weylin today yet either, what with
the crowds and the general uproar, but she knew he
was there somewhere, one of the fifty-six drivers entered in the Iditarod.

As usual, the mushers represented a variety of professions—medicine, law, real estate, electronics, carpentry, trapping, accounting—as well as many ethnic and national groups. The 1,100-mile-plus trip was a wilderness adventure with wide appeal. When the first Iditarod Trail Sled Dog Race to Nome was run in 1973, the mileage was set at 1,049 miles, since Alaska was the forty-ninth state, but in reality, the trail was longer, Jenna knew. She waited, tense with excitement and anticipation; she'd drawn the lowest starting number.

Not that it gave any real advantage; the differences in starting times would be accounted for when each musher took his or her mandatory twenty-four-hour layover somewhere along the trail.

And she wasn't number one. That starting position was reserved to the memory of Leonhard Seppala, hero of the diphtheria serum relay in 1925. His ashes rested along the trail. Jenna stood quietly while all present observed two minutes of silence for Seppala; then she spoke softly to Sonia and her team pulled up to the starting line.

Moments later she was off on the official trail through Anchorage, a trail that wound over snow-covered streets, bicycle paths, and sidewalks, before reaching the backwoods of Anchorage. The weather was uncomfortably warm for the dogs and even for her, since she had to pump to help the sled along some of the streets where the snow was scant. Crowds along the road called to her as she passed.

"Way to go, Red Riding Hood!"

"Nome, or don't come home, honey."

"Hey, Jenna, good luck."

The last was Emily, and Jenna smiled and waved to her.

Two hours later Jenna and her team were in Eagle and a Maki Equipment truck was waiting to take her, the dogs, and the sled across the bridges at the end of the Knik Arm of Cook Inlet to Wasilla, twenty-five miles away, where the real trail began.

An hour later she and the team were on their way to Knik. The week before, caches of dog and human food had been flown in by plane to the checkpoints along the trail to be used by the mushers as they reached these checkpoints.

Even without the extra food, her sled load was far from light. Race rules required a cold-weather sleeping bag, a hand ax, a pair of snowshoes, one day's food for each dog—at least two pounds per dog—a day's food for the driver, eight protective booties, made of canvas and Velcro, for each dog, and a packet of envelopes postmarked in Anchorage, later to be postmarked in Nome before being sold to raise money for the race.

All this equipment was verified at each checkpoint, and lack of any item disqualified the musher. But the sled also carried her two-burner camp stove, cooking pots, a change of clothes, spare footwear, repair tools, spare harness and gear, and an emergency medical kit for both the dogs and herself. She had also brought along a .38 Beretta, just in case she met belligerent wildlife. All told, her sled was carrying about two hundred pounds.

Jenna hoped to reach the first checkpoint at Susitna Station, about fifty miles to the west, before midnight. With her luck in the draw she headed the field and, although she'd been told that being in front didn't mean much in the early days of the race, it gave her a lift to be there.

The dogs, tongues lolling, trotted along a trail that snaked through leafless birch and alder groves and among stands of green-needled spruce. The temperature, in the teens, was still too warm for the huskies, and Jenna didn't push them. The terrain was relatively flat, but she was heading for the Alaska Range. To her north their tallest peak, Mount McKinley, thrust more than 20,000 feet into the almost cloudless blue sky. Denali, The Great One, the Alaskan Indians had named the peak. It was an awe-inspiring sight.

The next day she'd be cutting through the range at Rainy Pass, southwest of Mount McKinley, where the peaks were, thank God, not that high. Five to six thousand feet, the map said, and she'd go up to three thousand before dropping down into the pass. It would be a real challenge.

"Trail!" a man's voice called from behind her, the signal for her to stop her dogs and let the approaching team pass.

Startled, Jenna looked around quickly and saw a bearded musher, sun goggles on, the hood of his parka down, wearing a bright green cap. She didn't recognize him.

"Whoa," she ordered, and her dogs pulled to a halt, tongues hanging out, making the most of the chance to grab a few mouthfuls of snow. Sonia raised her muzzle and made a comment, in the typical husky "yow-owoo-oowoo," which would be a howl if the dog didn't keep opening and closing its mouth.

Jenna stared at the passing team. Wasn't that Chingo? She raised her sun goggles to get a better look. Her eyes flew to the man on the sled runners.

Weylin? She wouldn't have believed it if she hadn't seen it—Weylin with a full beard and mustache, dark, like his hair, and flecked with gray.

He saluted her as he passed her and she gazed after him, mouth agape. Weylin had certainly gotten carried away with his role as a musher. Did he think a beard would make him more Alaskan? Help him win the race?

She shook her head. Speed so early in the race wasn't productive and besides, it was too warm to push the dogs. He'd wear them out before he'd half begun.

Still, he was now running first.

Jenna fought down her impulse to urge her dogs to a faster pace. Let Weylin show off; she would travel easy because it was the right way to go. Time would tell who was the better musher, and she was confident it wouldn't be Weylin.

Wait until he hit those tough switchbacks that led up to Rainy Pass the next day. Wait until he had to drop a thousand feet in five miles on a trail that was nothing but an ice chute. Rainy Pass wasn't for *cheechakos*.

Thinking about the pass made her a bit tense. But she'd make it. She and the dogs.

Weylin laughed aloud as Jenna's team dropped behind him. She'd been the front runner and he'd passed her. He was ahead. Respects to old Seppala, but Weylin Matthews was number one in this year's race.

Now all he had to do was stay ahead. Oh, there'd be tough miles coming up. He'd heard all about the perils of Rainy Pass; the dangers of losing the trail; how, even in zero temperatures or below, there could be overflow on the frozen rivers that could freeze the dogs' feet and cripple them.

"Trust your dogs," he'd been warned. "Especially your leader. Nine out of ten times on the trail he knows more than you do."

"We'll win this damn thing, Chingo," Weylin muttered. "Show those females back there that no matter how good they think they are, you and I are better."

Nine

As her team trotted through the pass, the steep blue-white sides of the mountains to either side seemed to Jenna to rise forever into the clouds. The trail followed Pass Fork and then Dalzell Creek, winding through the canyon until it reached the Tatina River. At that point she had to worry about overflow, a danger in late winter when water begins to trickle into river bottoms, where its flow is blocked by the river ice, causing the water to flow up and on top of the ice.

Overflow freezes to dogs' feet, to mushers' boots, and to sled runners and, even worse, it hides holes in the ice. At the Tatina, the wind had swept snow away so that much of the surface was glare ice with no traction for the dogs or the sled. But since the hot pink of the surveyor's tape that marked the trail was laid onto the ice, Jenna had no choice but to follow where it led. Her team slid and scrabbled on toward the Rohn River checkpoint, the sled skidding behind with Jenna praying they wouldn't encounter a hidden hole.

She saw no sign of Weylin, so she decided he must have negotiated that stretch without problems. When she reached the Rohn Roadhouse, the checkers confirmed that he'd passed by a half hour before.

Still first. She was second, and she'd caught glimpses of at least three other mushers behind her.

She headed north from the checkpoint, the trail following more frozen rivers with puddled overflow. Jenna worried about the huskies, although, unlike humans, dogs can get wet and will dry and warm up while continuing to run. Still, the soaking did their feet no good. She breathed a sigh of relief when the trail left the last river and plunged into stands of thick spruce that later gave way to thinner alder thickets, then spruce again.

Now that they were over the Alaska Range and into the great Interior, the weather grew colder. The thermometer hovered at just above zero, making better weather for mushing. She should reach Farewell about dark or soon after. She'd be three hundred miles from Anchorage by then and quite ready to enjoy the first hot running water since she'd hit the trail, Farewell being a flight service station with modern facilities. With rivers the only roads in most of the Interior, planes were a necessity.

She'd catch up to Weylin at Farewell, no doubt about it. All the mushers stopped for at least a couple of hours there to wash, use the clothes dryers, and feed their dogs. The three teams behind her would also catch up.

Sonia had obeyed every command, all the dogs were behaving, and all were healthy. If everything contin-

ued to go well she'd reach Nikolai before the end of the
fifth day. At that rate she just might come in first.

As she congratulated herself, she noticed the dogs'
ears prick forward. Alerted, she strained to see ahead.
Before she could make out what interested the animals, the sled lurched forward so quickly she almost
lost her grip on the drive bow. The dogs were off—
they paid no attention to her shouts but kept on running at full tilt. She had all she could do to hang on.

From under the spruce trees to the right, a cloud of
white fluttered and rose, and it took her a moment to
realize she was looking at a flock of winter-white
ptarmigans flushed by her team.

The birds flew low and the dogs raced on in mad
pursuit, plunging, despite the brake, into the trees to
the left of the trail after the ptarmigans.

"Whoa! Sonia, whoa!" Jenna called.

The sled careened wildly on.

Jenna knew huskies could get really cranked up
chasing wildlife, but she'd somehow thought Sonia
above such canine shenanigans. She'd been wrong.
Certainly Sonia was paying no attention to Jenna's
commands and was leading the other dogs farther and
farther off the trail as she strained to catch the birds.

Jenna, hanging grimly to the handlebar, struggled
to grab the snow hook without falling off. She managed to get a hand on it, swung the pronged end out,
and was lucky enough to hook it around the trunk of
a spruce. The huskies were brought up short. Jenna
leaped from the sled, holding it back to avoid hitting
the dogs. She whipped out the jangler and shook it to
get their attention.

Sonia turned to look at her, tongue lolling out, the
husky grin intact. "What's all the fuss?" she seemed

to be asking. "Can't a dog have a little fun now and then?"

Jenna stalked to the front of the team. "Now hear this," she said firmly. "We're heading back to the trail, and we'll follow it from now on. To Nome."

Not one dog looked repentant. When she retrieved the hook, climbed on the runners, and ordered Sonia to "Come gee," the lead dog obediently made the 180-degree turn to the right and they followed their own tracks back to the trail. Some minutes later they were once again heading for Farewell, but Jenna couldn't be certain one of the teams behind her hadn't had the chance to get ahead.

Her annoyance at Sonia gradually faded. The leader hadn't been deliberately defying her as Chingo had done. No. Sonia had simply reacted to the birds as any dog might have done, with the enthusiastic support of the rest of the team. They were dogs, after all, not humans.

The moon was up, half-full, by the time Jenna spotted the red lights she'd been told to look for at the tops of the radio and navigation towers at the end of Farewell's airstrip. Once in the settlement, she had time to see that there was only one dog team curled up in the snow outside a frame building before photographers' bulbs began to flash.

One of the hazards of the race, she'd discovered, was media personnel who had been flown into the larger checkpoints. Some thought nothing of interrupting while dogs were being fed and sometimes even woke sleeping mushers to interview them.

"Any comments, Ms Henderson," a TV newsman asked, "on the fact that the first two teams are Maki Equipment dogs?"

"We feed them a secret California formula," she managed to say lightly as she stretched out her gang line and set the snow hook so the dogs would stay put. They knew by then what it meant when they stopped near a building and immediately lay down to rest.

After she'd checked in with the Iditarod official, Jenna found her cache of dog food and made her way to the building pointed out to her as the laundry. The heat inside hit her like a blow.

"What took you so long?" Weylin asked from the floor where he sat by his camp stove stirring a pot of dog food.

He was stripped of parka, overalls, and boots and looked lean and handsome in a red wool shirt and black pants. What she could see of his face was tan, and he looked fit and healthy, even clean—while she felt absolutely filthy and was so tired she could hardly stand.

"You grew a beard!" she said accusingly. "You once told me that wasn't for you."

"Dog racing wasn't for me then either. One seems to go with the other." He stroked the beard. "Except for icing up a bit from my breath, it does tend to keep my face warm."

He's proud of the damn thing, she thought. Actually, the beard and mustache did nothing to detract from his looks; they only gave him a more rugged cast that added to his appeal. Not that she intended to tell him.

"Your picture will be all over the papers," she said, "coming into Farewell first."

"On Anchorage TV too. They interviewed me. I said I owed it all to Chingo."

"You just might."

"I knew that's what the Alaskan folks like to hear, and he *is* one dog in a million. No slackers on his team." Weylin stopped stirring the food, rose, and took a step toward her.

Jenna resisted the impulse to back away.

"You look beat," he said. "You ought to get some sleep here."

"And let you get farther ahead? No thanks." Jenna yanked off her parka and began unfastening her coveralls, not only because the heat in the room was stifling, but it gave her something to do other than look at Weylin.

The door swung open and two more mushers pushed inside, both older men. They glanced from Weylin to Jenna and the taller one, a man named Charlie Jones, said, "Hear we might get a storm in the next couple of days."

"Is that right?" Weylin asked, frowning.

Jenna didn't know whether to believe Charlie or not. Some drivers were notorious for trying to psych out other racers. Setting up her stove, she opened her gunnysack of food.

"Yessir, a storm'll sure separate the men from the boys," Charlie went on. "The men from the women too."

Jenna ignored the comment, determined not to let him get her goat. In a bad storm no musher put his dogs on the trail, and Charlie knew that as well as she did.

"You use a whip much?" Charlie asked Weylin.

"To threaten. Haven't had to use one on a dog yet."

"I'll bet the little lady here has never whipped a dog in her life." Charlie's tone was jocular.

"Ms Henderson doesn't believe in hitting dogs," Weylin said after it became apparent Jenna didn't intend to answer. "Her training methods work well for her; she's got a great team. Going to be hard to beat."

"Not in the long run." Charlie spoke positively. "Now, I don't have a thing against women trainers and mushers, not a thing. They do right well in speed racing. Occasionally one does okay in the Iditarod even wins like Libby Riddles. Overall though, on a long bastard like this race, a woman's not going to win. You see, they don't believe in the notion that you can't drive a dog to death. It's the truth, you can't. The dog'll quit first. So, anyway, women are too softhearted to drive dogs really hard, and that's what wins this race. Ain't that so, Bucky?"

The other man shrugged. "Whatever wins, wins."

Jenna's eyes widened as she recognized Bucky Nagord, favored to win this Iditarod. Regardless of what she'd said to Weylin, she'd been toying with the idea of grabbing a couple of hours' sleep at Farewell when she'd fed the dogs, eaten, and gotten herself and a few clothes clean. After listening to Charlie and seeing such dangerous competition so close behind, she decided she'd skip the sleep and take the dogs on toward Nikolai. She'd been told there was spruce forest for the first stretch of the forty-five miles. Good camping; she could even build a fire. And she'd be alone; she'd avoid all the Charlies and get a jump on the others as well. She'd avoid Weylin too; she was so aware of his every movement that it was difficult to keep her mind on what she was doing.

She turned to Charlie with a demure smile. "Why, I haven't been worrying my little old head about how to stay in front, not at all. I just know you chivalrous gentlemen would always allow a lady to go first.'' She batted her eyes a couple of times, then picked up a pail to get water for her dogs.

As she went out she heard Weylin laugh.

When Jenna broke camp at one in the morning and set off again, the northern lights, spreading green and yellow banners across the sky, were so bright she could see the dogs' shadows on the snow. It was ten below, and she could feel the ice crystals form and melt in her nostrils as she breathed.

By dawn she'd left the spruce forest and come to the Burn, where in the summer of 1977, a wildfire had roared across 361,000 acres of trees and brush. No second growth was large enough yet to break the wind, and the snow gusted in front of her, doing its best to erase the trail while also burying the pink surveyor's tape marking the way.

"Okay, Sonia, it's up to you," she muttered as she started across the Burn. Sonia would be able to feel the hard snow—packed down by snow machines for the trail—under the drifted snow as she ran. At least, Jenna hoped so. She had to trust her leader; there was no way she could be sure they were headed right.

Over her right shoulder, to the southeast, the tall peaks of the Alaska Range caught the first of the sun's rays, turning the snow glorious shades of pink. In the distance ahead were the lower peaks of the Kuskokwim Mountains. Also ahead but closer, she saw multiple big black mounds to the left and she stared, trying to make out what she was looking at. Then she remembered.

Buffalo. In the 1930's, buffalo had been introduced into the Interior, and the herd had prospered and grown. She searched her mind for anything she'd ever read about the great beasts. All she could recall was some old Western movie that showed a buffalo stampede.

She had a momentary vision of hundreds of buffalo racing toward her and the dogs, of being trampled under sharp hooves. No, she admonished herself, don't be foolish. Why would they stampede? But she couldn't rid herself of the thought, and she kept a wary eye on them until her team had left the herd behind.

Despite the sun, the wind made running unpleasant, and both Jenna and the dogs were glad to leave the Burn behind for river ice, even with the overflow problems. She was more than ready for a rest when she spotted the three crosses atop the peak of Nikolai's Russian Orthodox Church. The dogs speeded up as they always did when approaching a settlement.

Schoolchildren ran to greet her as she urged the dogs toward the checkpoint.

"Red Riding Hood," they shouted, "you're second."

So someone was ahead of her. Weylin? Or one of the others? She stopped and gave the dogs a snack. The huskies' footpads looked in good condition, but the checker had told her that between Nikolai and McGrath the trail was punchy and icy. Without protection, that would be hard on the dogs' feet so she put the canvas booties on all thirteen. She also found out it was not Weylin ahead of her but the top contender, Bucky.

McGrath was forty-five miles to the west. It was the hub of air traffic in the Interior, a bustling rural town. There she planned to take her mandatory twenty-four-hour layover. As she left the log cabins of Nikolai behind her for turns and twists of the Kuskokwim River, she couldn't help wondering what had happened to Weylin. Had he stayed in Farewell for his layover? If so, he was still in the running, because she hadn't heard that Bucky had taken his mandatory layover yet. She really hadn't expected Weylin to do so well, hadn't even expected him to get this far.

If Charlie and Bucky hadn't come into the laundry room when they did, what had Weylin intended to do? Kiss her? Hold her? She wouldn't have let him, but perversely, she'd longed to have him touch her. Whenever she saw him there was always the same leap of excitement, the same sudden joy. She couldn't help wondering what he felt.

She'd looked tired, he'd said. She *was* tired. And she'd be even more tired before the race was over.

McGrath, Ophir, Iditarod. At Iditarod she was halfway to Nome. "Iditarod" came from an Indian word meaning distant place, and she could understand the name. There the last great gold rush in Alaska had taken place, Jenna knew, but except for a few hardy souls it was now a ghost town. She was surrounded by miles of uninhabited wilderness and for the first time felt real fear. What was she doing out there behind a team of huskies, one of two women braving the cold and the trail?

The rasping "shush" of the sled runners, the steady rush of wind, and the creaking of the stanchions combined with the feel of the handlebar under her hands and the runners beneath her feet to reassure her. She was there because she wanted to be; it was a testing, and she meant to measure up.

After they'd all passed through Iditarod, Weylin and Bucky were both ahead of her. The three of them made the sixty-five mile crossing to Shageluk in less than twelve hours. Charlie was close behind, coming into the village as Jenna pulled out.

On to Anvik and then north up the Yukon River, the Mississippi of Alaska, for 140 miles of river trail, through Grayling to Kaltag. Jenna became convinced that this last stretch was the worst part of the run, with a thirty-knot wind howling across the river ice and the temperature at twenty below. Occasionally she would get off the runners and run to keep up the dogs' morale.

At Kaltag she ate beaver stew and bought beaver meat from a trapper for her dogs. Bucky was there, but Weylin had gone on.

"He don't sleep," Bucky told her. "The guy's gonna crash pretty soon. Hope he don't fall off the sled and freeze."

Once again she put booties on her dogs for the run to Unalakleet, on Norton Sound, part of the Bering Sea. That was Eskimo country, and the Kaltag portage was centuries old, used by Indians and Eskimos before white men ever came to Alaska. It was the twelfth day of the race, and it took her sixteen miserable hours to cross the low mountains, snow blowing into both her and the dogs' faces. On the run down to the coast, she passed Bucky and finally caught up to Weylin.

"Trail!" she called as her team edged up behind him. He kept on. "Trail!" she shouted again. He didn't stop.

Angry, Jenna shook her jangler as she shouted his name, repeating, "Trail, trail!"

Weylin looked back and called, "Whoa!" His team stopped and Jenna pulled around him. As she went by on the sled he saluted her much as he'd done on the day he passed her.

After she'd pulled well ahead of him it occurred to her that his not stopping at her first call might not have been deliberate. Bucky had said Weylin wasn't stopping to sleep. He might have been in a semisomnolent daze; she'd experienced the feeling herself.

A musher could push himself and still rest his dogs, because the dogs could lie down, and usually did, every time the sled came to a halt. The musher had to bustle around thawing their food and water and feeding them, but the dogs could sleep while he worked. By this stage of the race, no driver was getting enough sleep, but Weylin could be allowing himself even less rest in his determination to be first.

Someone ought to warn him. She glanced behind her, but his team was out of sight. Jenna shrugged. He wouldn't listen to her anyway. If she did stop and wait for him, he'd just grasp the chance to take the lead again.

Stubborn alpha male.

Between Unalakleet and Shaktoolik she camped along the trail. The weather was warmer on the coast—ten above zero—but there were no trees, hence no wood to burn and no spruce boughs for the dogs to lie on. She chose a leeward spot behind a low hill, set up the camp stove, and began to cook the dogs' food.

I'm going to come in first, she told herself as she stirred the pot, but she was too tired to feel any emotion. Once she was finished with the dogs and sure they were bedded down, she heated some fried chicken she'd had flown into Unalakleet and chewed it down to the bone before crawling into her sleeping bag.

The dogs woke her, snarling and yapping like crazy. She waited for a moment, trying to decide whether they were commenting on some passing wildlife or defending the camp against it. As she started to struggle to a sitting position, a pointed muzzle thrust itself into her face.

Wolf, she thought in terror, cringing away.

A tongue came out and licked her face, and she let her pent-up breath whoosh out. One of the huskies, loose. She should have realized that. For all she knew there weren't any wolves on the coast; she hadn't heard them at night since she had crossed the Kuskokwims.

Sighing, she edged out of the bag and reached for the dog. She ought to be glad the husky had chosen to wake her rather than taking off into the wilds as they were prone to do. If she lost a dog she'd be disqualified.

The moon was up, almost full. She looked to see what time it was. Three in the morning. Then she tried to identify the dog she held. Was it Yetse, one of the wheelers? Pulling him with her, she stumbled toward the still yapping huskies and did a head count.

Thirteen. No, she must have counted wrong.

Thirteen again. She stared down at the animal she had by the ruff. Someone else's dog. The dark face looked familiar.

With a rush of apprehension she recognized him. Chingo.

What was he doing in her camp?

Sonia was there, of course. If Chingo had worked himself loose, he'd certainly head straight for Sonia if he could find her. That must be what had happened. Weylin, careless because he was exhausted, hadn't secured Chingo well enough.

"What am I going to do with you?" she asked Chingo.

He gazed up at her, his slanted eyes dark and incommunicative.

Weylin could forfeit the race if he didn't recover Chingo. Well, she certainly wasn't going to break camp and haul her dogs back along the trail to return Chingo to Weylin. She couldn't, though, trust that the husky, if turned loose, would go back to Weylin.

On the other hand, she couldn't take Chingo with her, because the rules didn't allow a musher to have any dogs but his or her own, and she'd end up forfeiting.

What to do?

She could chain Chingo next to the trail, where Weylin couldn't possibly miss seeing him. Maybe she could find a piece of that pink tape to tie to his collar.

Chingo whined at her feet, pulling to free himself from her grip. He wants to get to Sonia, she thought sympathetically. Except he could have been with Sonia and he'd roused her instead. Odd behavior for a dog, especially since Chingo hadn't been all that fond of her. Icy fingers of fear brushed Jenna's spine.

Was something wrong with Weylin?

She shook her head. He wouldn't send a dog for help; that was ridiculous. These were sled dogs, whose job was to mush, and a leader was just that—a leader. Chingo was no pet, and this wilderness wasn't a place where you could order a dog to "go home." Weylin would know that a husky turned loose might go anywhere, might even go permanently wild.

No, Weylin wouldn't have freed Chingo to go for help.

But what if Weylin was in trouble? Helpless? Chingo could well have gotten loose. Of course, nothing at all might be wrong with Weylin and Chingo still could have broken free. Was she looking for trouble where none existed?

But the damn dog had shoved his muzzle in her face. Why?

If she hooked up her dogs and backtracked to try to find Weylin, she'd lose her lead, since she couldn't have more than half an hour's advantage as it was. No, she wouldn't go back; she'd chain Chingo by the trail and take off for Shaktoolik immediately. It would be full daylight by the time she had to cross the Norton Bay ice to Koyuk. Then it was only Elim, Golovin, White Mountain, and Port Safety before Nome. She'd be first to come in, and to hell with Weylin and Charlie and all the others who thought a woman could win the Iditarod only by a fluke.

Jenna nodded and, still with a firm grip on Chingo, found an extra chain in her gear. Once he was secured, she gave the dogs a snack, intending to stop along the trail later to feed and water them properly. She gave Chingo a ball of her special tallow, cheese, and vitamin mix, and he gulped it down so hungrily she offered him another. It seemed he had not been fed the night before.

The thought nagged her as she stowed her gear on the sled and hitched up her team. Leaving the snow hook holding them, she walked Chingo down to the trail and pounded in one of her long stakes with the butt of her ax, then chained him to it. She slogged back to her dogs, still worrying.

Chingo wouldn't have run off from Weylin's camp if he was hungry; he'd have waited to be fed. Huskies were as smart as any other dog and knew where their food came from.

Come on, Jenna, she chided herself. Most likely Weylin's sleeping peacefully back in Unalakleet, where the villagers opened their homes to the mushers. If you backtrail he'll laugh at you. He certainly wouldn't give up *his* chance of being first for anything or anybody.

Jenna stepped on the runners. "Hike!" she called to Sonia, then, "Haw," steering her onto the trail leading to Nome.

As they pulled away, Chingo sent up a mournful howl and Sonia slowed down.

"Hike!" Jenna called again. "No nonsense, Sonia. We aren't stopping because of Chingo."

Sonia broke into the trail trot.

And we aren't going back because of Weylin either, Jenna told herself firmly.

Ten

Chingo had done her a favor in waking her up, Jenna decided. Otherwise she might have slept on and lost her edge. To her left the open water of Norton Sound glittered under the moon. To the east, on her right, barren snow-covered hills rose in front of the higher Whalebacks behind them. A beautiful, if desolate, sight.

She might have been the only human on earth.

How lonesome that would be. As lonesome as a world without Weylin.

All the fears she'd been repressing rose, dark phantoms flitting through her mind. Weylin ill, unable to care for himself. Injured. Lost and off the trail, without his dogs and sled.

What did coming in first matter if something had happened to him? What did anything matter without him?

I love him, she thought in wonder. Only him. It makes no difference how he feels about me, I love Weylin. I have from the first. I always will. Why did I think I had a choice? You don't choose to love; it happens and there's nothing you can do to stop it.

"Come gee!" she shouted to Sonia.

Immediately the lead dog pulled to the right, making a U-turn. The other dogs followed, then the sled.

"Hike!"

Sonia, aware she was heading back toward Chingo, broke into a lope and the sled picked up speed, runners slashing through the snow.

When they came near the chained dog, Sonia slowed down without being told, finally coming to a halt. Jenna jumped off the sled and, hastily rigging a harness, hitched Chingo into lead position beside Sonia, as they used to run.

"Hike!" she called to him, hoping he'd lead her to Weylin.

She no longer cared if she found him warm and comfortable, sleeping in Unalakleet. In fact, she wished she could be sure of finding him there, because it would mean he wasn't in danger. She couldn't go on without knowing where and how he was.

The fourteen huskies pulled her at a fast lope. Every moment she expected to see another team headed toward her and hoped against hope it would be Weylin's. She swallowed repeatedly, trying to dislodge the cold lump of dread that stuck in her throat.

They crossed a frozen creek bed, and Chingo suddenly veered off the trail and to the left, following the stream toward the hills. Jenna's hands clenched on the drive bow. She'd known all along Weylin wasn't in Unalakleet.

Steady, she warned herself. He might be perfectly fine, cozy in his sleeping bag, nothing wrong.

A small building loomed ahead of them, and dogs set up a clamor. Chingo slowed down, stopping beside what Jenna saw was a dilapidated metal shack. Probably an Eskimo fishing house, she thought, used for spring salmon runs. She leaped off the sled, hurriedly stretched out the gang line, and set her snow hook.

"Weylin?" she called.

No answer.

She strode toward the shack. Beyond the building his team was hitched to the sled, a snow hook in place. When they recognized her smell, most of the huskies quieted and lay down. Behind her, Chingo whined.

There was no door. Jenna drew in her breath when she saw a dark shape huddled on the dirt floor just inside. She ran toward the door, crying, "Weylin! Weylin!"

He didn't move or answer. She knelt beside him. He had on all his winter gear and was lying prone, his face turned to one side. No sleeping bag. The temperature had dropped to three degrees above zero. How long had he been like that?

"Weylin," she cried again, shaking him. "Wake up, Weylin."

No response.

Desperately she yanked off one of her mitts and tried to find a pulse in his neck, sliding cold fingers under his parka, her heart in her mouth as she fumbled to find the right place.

Was that a throb she felt? It was so faint she could hardly tell.

Hypothermia. How did you treat hypothermia, the awful numbing cold stroke that crept up on the unwary in winter? Heat, first of all and most important. She couldn't build a fire; there was no wood for fuel, and even the shack was metal. The camp stoves were built for cooking, not heating.

She could start up a stove, heat water for tea.

Not enough, and what if she couldn't rouse him to drink?

Sleeping bags, she thought feverishly. His and mine. Racing first to her sled, then to his, she grabbed the sleeping gear and hurried back to the hut. Laying his bivvy bag on the dirt floor of the hut, she managed to roll him over onto it. She flung his sleeping bag and hers on top of him and bent close.

"Weylin," she said urgently. "You have to wake up; you have to help me. Please, Weylin, oh, please wake up."

He made a sound deep in his throat, but his eyes didn't open. She shook him again, removing a mitt to slap him with her bare hand. He had to get inside a sleeping bag; having them thrown over him wasn't nearly enough.

Even inside his bag, his own temperature might already have dropped too low for his reflected body heat to warm him.

"Weylin." She moaned, putting her face to his. "I love you. I don't want to lose you. Listen to me and wake up."

He moved. She felt his eyelids flutter.

"It's Jenna," she said. "We've got to get you inside your sleeping bag. Help me."

He rolled onto his side and tried to sit up. He was confused and incoherent, but with constant urging she managed to get his boots off and then his parka. Finally he was in his sleeping bag, which she had first managed to enclose within the bivvy bag. Hurriedly she pulled off her own boots and parka and eased herself inside next to him. Her physical warmth was the only heat she had to offer him.

Snuggling next to his coldness, she put her arms around him. After a few minutes she thought, *No, this won't do it. His clothes prevent warmth from reaching him; we've got to be skin to skin for my body to warm his.*

Obviously neither of them could get out of the sleeping bag to disrobe. After a struggle, Jenna managed to unbutton Weylin's shirt, remove his belt, unzip his pants, and shove them down. He still had on thermal underwear, and she pushed the top up and the bottoms down as best she could. It wasn't much easier to get her own clothes off, and she wound up like Weylin—more or less undressed.

Still, flesh touched flesh, breast to chest and thigh to thigh. She shivered at the coolness of his skin despite the fact that she'd begun to perspire from her exertion. Jenna wrapped her arms about him and hugged him as tightly as she could.

"You'll be fine, you'll be all right," she murmured.

For a long time he said nothing, lying passive against her warmth. She grew drowsy and her eyes closed.

"Jenna." He spoke in a whisper. "Jenna?"

She came awake immediately. "Yes, I'm here, Weylin."

"No."

"It's Jenna. Here with you."

"Why not on the trail?" His words slurred a little. "Ahead. You're ahead. First."

"I came to take care of you, Weylin. Don't worry. Rest."

"Shouldn't be here. You shouldn't. Nome. You'd come in first in Nome."

"Never mind the race; it's not important."

"Winning's important." His voice was stronger. "You can win. Go on."

"I don't care about winning, I care about you. Did you send Chingo to look for me?"

"Chingo? He could have won. I failed him. You still have a chance, you can win for me."

"No," she said. "I'm staying here. You've got to get warm. Don't you understand, Weylin? You almost—" she broke off, unable to bring herself to say the word. "Do you remember what happened?" she finished.

"Tired. So damn tired. Cold."

Exhaustion had crept up on him, she decided. He'd collapsed before he could set up camp, oblivious to the danger of lying in the cold.

"You're beginning to warm up," she told him. "Soon you'll feel better. Rest. Go to sleep."

"Failed," he muttered. "I failed."

"What difference does the race make? You're alive, that's what matters."

"All right. I'm all right. You go on."

She understood he didn't realize the seriousness of what had happened to him. He was still confused by the effects of the hypothermia.

"Shh, don't talk any more." She spoke as though to a child. "Close your eyes. It's time to go to sleep."

He sighed and his arms came around her. A few minutes later his deepened breathing told her he slept. Her own eyelids drooped closed. As she began to drift off she smiled, thinking drowsily that she'd never have believed it if anyone had told her she'd be this close to Weylin and not be able to stay awake, that all either of them would want to do was sleep.

She dreamed she was on the trail, the dogs running, running, racing against time. Where they were headed she wasn't sure, knowing that she must get there before it was too late.

Something moved on the trail ahead, huge animals, hundreds of them cutting across the trail, blocking it so the dogs could pass neither in front nor in back of the herd. Sonia plunged ahead in a frenzy, determined to pull the sled into the midst of the giant animals.

"Whoa!" Jenna tried to scream, but no sound came. Closer and closer the sled came to the buffalo. The dogs disappeared among the stampeding herd, swallowed up, and if she didn't jump soon it would be her turn; she'd be crushed under the hooves of the buffalo.

Jenna leaped from the sled, seeing too late that someone lay in the basket—Weylin was in the sled's basket and was doomed....

"No!" she cried. "No, no!"

"Jenna," someone murmured. She struggled to come awake, to free herself of the nightmare. "Jenna, Jenna, what's the matter?"

Her eyes flew open to pitch darkness. Where was she?

"Jenna?"

Weylin! She clutched him, shreds of the dream still clouding her mind. From somewhere nearby a dog yipped, then quieted.

Reality wiped away the traces of nightmare. The race. Weylin. Under her hands his skin was very warm. Warm and smooth. An electric tingle quivered along her spine.

"All right now?" he asked.

"I had a bad dream. How are you?"

"I'm not sure how we came to be together. All I recall is bits and pieces. Are the dogs—"

"They're fine. Chingo came to get me; that's why I'm here."

"I think he licked my face once. Everything's distorted. Did I pass out?"

"Yes."

"And you found me, got me into the bag. Hypothermia?"

"You were well on your way into it. I couldn't think of any other way to warm you up."

"Nothing wrong with this one." He pulled her closer, his beard soft against her face.

She could feel his arousal beginning, but he only held her, neither kissing nor caressing her. She lay quietly in his arms, but desire simmered within her, diffusing sweetly through her veins.

"Jenna?" His breath was warm and moist in her ear. "You know I want you. I can't help myself with you so close to me. God knows I've wanted you since the night we met. But you didn't crawl into my sleeping bag to be made love to."

No, she hadn't. And she understood what he was telling her. He wouldn't take advantage of the situation.

Oh, Weylin, I love you so much, she yearned to say. You're the man I dreamed of for all these years. Why has it taken me so long to realize it?

Jenna said nothing. Instead, she lifted her hands to his face and turned it until her lips touched him. She kissed his mouth, his eyelids, his forehead and then his lips again, her tongue slipping delicately between them.

Weylin drew in his breath, pulling away a little. "Jenna, if you go on—"

She put her fingers over his mouth, pressing herself against the hard length of his body. He groaned and clasped her to him, his lips covering hers, his tongue enfolding hers. Her breasts flattened against his chest, the crisp curl of his chest hair teasing her nipples.

His maleness throbbed against her thigh and, inside her, responsive muscles contracted in anticipation, sending flurries of erotic expectation into her loins.

My man, she thought bemusedly. That's what he is; Weylin is mine. For as long as tonight lasts, he's mine.

She needed to touch him, to learn him, to caress every part of him she could reach. Her fingers crept between them, finding his tiny, hard masculine nipples, following the exciting path of hair that led from his chest downward, a path that flared into a thicket of warm, springy hair.

Weylin groaned and tried to pull her closer, but she resisted, her hand dipping lower in its journey of discovery. She heard her heart thundering in her ears as she touched him.

"Jenna." His voice was hoarse. "Do you know what you're doing?"

"I'm making love to you," she whispered.

As his body shuddered under her continuing caresses, his fingers found her breasts and stroked them, gently pinching the taut nipples to pleasurable need.

His head bent until his mouth was at one breast, then the other, his hands stroking downward, sending erotic electric impulses along the sensitive skin of her abdomen. She cried out softly as he penetrated her secret recess with his fingers, his delicate touch adding fuel to her increasing desire, a desire now burning out of control.

Heat. Moisture. Pulsating tension. Thrilling jolts of rapture. She couldn't begin to describe the sensations that roiled inside her, demanding release.

"Weylin," she breathed. "Please..." Her voice trailed off, unsure exactly what she was asking for.

"Who's making love to whom?" he growled.

Her passion for him was ferocious, animallike in its overwhelming intensity and overpowering need. Yet the gentleness of love that was intermixed, love for this wolf of a man she'd chosen. The future didn't matter, there was only now. Only Weylin. She and Weylin together.

He kissed her, his body moving over hers. Their lips melded as he eased her thighs apart. She felt him poised at the threshold of her womanhood and arched to him, unable to control her wild need.

"Please," she moaned, clinging to him, feeling the trembling tension of his arms as he supported himself above her. "I want you, I want all of you."

He entered her slowly, probing and withdrawing until she whimpered in sweet agony, a roaring in her ears, her body throbbing in a delirium of longing. She writhed against him, her fingers digging into his shoulders.

Suddenly he thrust hard, and she felt a piercing joy as he filled her. The ecstasy of his long, slow strokes started a tremor deep within her that grew and grew until she was possessed by a frenzied drive to be closer to him, to become a part of him; her body, his body; her heart, his heart.

She loved him, had always loved him, would always love him.

He was as wild and wonderful as this country she loved, difficult, demanding, and dangerous. But she'd dared the challenge and she wondered why she'd ever feared to love him. No other man could ever have made her feel like this; no other man ever would.

His mouth claimed hers in a deep, demanding kiss and she lost herself, her senses blurring in the mindless need that engulfed her. Perspiration slicked her body and his as they joined in an ever-quickening rhythm that raised her up and up, higher than any peak, above the great mountain of Denali, up beyond the fiery flash of the aurora, until the sun's glowing charge exploded within her, fragmenting her.

At that moment she cried out, heard Weylin's gasping, matching cry and knew he was with her, two luminous spirits in a place beyond the world, a place they'd discovered together.

Jenna floated down as lazily as a snowflake. She drifted in an afterglow of pleasure, warm and satiated. Next to her she felt Weylin sigh and relax.

Yet it wasn't over. She snuggled next to him, content to feel the warmth of his body, the soft brush of his beard against her face. She slept.

Weylin woke with a start. For long moments he was disoriented, unable to understand the sensation of pleasurable fatigue or the wonderful warmth that surrounded him.

There'd been darkness and cold. Then a radiant white light that had both frightened and drawn him at the same time. It seemed to him his grandmother had been there, smiling and beckoning. He'd loved Grandma Kate, and he knew she loved him. But she'd left him, gone away like the mother he'd once loved.

Grandma Kate was dead. How could she be smiling at him?

He'd wanted to bask in his grandmother's smile, to go with her, but someone kept calling his name. Calling him back. He'd been whirled away from the radiant light and Grandma Kate, thrust into cold and darkness again.

Then there'd been a kaleidoscope of sensation. Warmth. The marvel of a woman's body pressed to his. Jenna's body. The incredible rush of passion as she'd bent to him, let him love her.

He was dreaming.

No.

He was in his sleeping bag and someone was with him. Jenna was with him. How could that be?

She was there, he couldn't deny it. Despite the darkness he knew the feel of her, and her intoxicating scent filled his nostrils. He'd made love to her. The memory of joining with her overwhelmed him.

Jenna, Jenna. No woman had ever stirred him as she had. The wonder of her choked him. How could he ever be satisfied with anyone but Jenna again?

He slid his hand over the curve of her hip, her skin smooth and satiny under his fingers. She shifted in her sleep, cuddling closer, and desire rose in him again.

At the same time he experienced the renewed need for her, he also fought against a vast lethargy that threatened to consume him. He'd never been so tired in all his life.

From somewhere nearby an animal howled, and Weylin tensed. Where the hell was he? Dogs. The race. He was competing in the Iditarod. So was Jenna. She was ahead of him. No, she was in this sleeping bag with him.

Suddenly he remembered. She'd come back. She'd said Chingo had gotten loose to her. She'd back-tracked, following Chingo.

To save me, Weylin told himself. Hypothermia. She'd roused him from what would have been a fatal sleep, forced him into his sleeping bag, and crawled in with him to warm him. He blinked, wide awake at last. Had Jenna given up her chance to win the Iditarod because of him?

He grasped her shoulder, shaking her gently. "Jenna, wake up."

"Weylin?" She spoke sleepily, nuzzling her lips against his neck.

"How long have you been with me?"

She moved her face away from his. "With you? I'm not certain. Several hours at the least. Why?"

He ignored the question. "How far ahead of me were you?"

"I don't know exactly—five miles or so."

"No one in front of you?"

"Not when I made camp. And I don't think anyone passed me after that."

"You still might make it if Bucky stayed in Una-lakleet. Charlie hadn't come in yet when I left town, and no one else was close." Urgency threaded through his voice. "You have to get going, get out of here in a hurry."

She didn't say anything.

"Jenna, don't you understand? You still can win."

"How do you feel?"

"I'm okay. Fine. Don't worry about me—go on."

"When did you eat last?"

"I had something in Unalakleet when I gave the dogs their snack. We're wasting time talking when you should be moving."

"You need food. You need a good long sleep in a warm house. Unalakleet's the closest."

"I'll manage, Jenna."

She twisted away from him, but not far; there wasn't enough room in the bag. "I'm not leaving until I can see for myself you're able to go on alone."

"I'll prove it," he said impatiently, ignoring the lassitude that dragged at him. "We'll break camp now. I'll show you."

To Weylin's surprise and annoyance, once he was dressed and out of the sleeping bag, he found his legs were the consistency of overdone spaghetti. He had to steady himself against the frame of the doorway to put on his parka, had to sit on the bag to pull on his boots.

The sky was graying with dawn, and the dim light showed him Jenna's concerned gaze.

"I'm fine," he muttered.

She didn't argue; she simply said, "We'll feed the dogs first."

"Don't you care if you win?" he demanded.

"Some things are more important than coming in first in a race. Can you light your stove?"

He wanted to shake some sense into her. He rose, trying to conceal his stagger as he walked toward her.

When he put his mittened hands on her shoulders it was more for support than any other reason.

How dark and mysterious her eyes were in the dawn glimmer. For a moment he forgot everything but Jenna and the way she'd felt in his arms.

The dogs, hearing them, began to yip, and Jenna turned away. "They're hungry, and so am I."

After three tries he finally got the stove lit, but by the time he'd managed to find the dog food he was so exhausted he had to sit on the sled and rest. He closed his eyes for an instant; the next thing he knew, Jenna was standing over him, calling his name.

"Weylin!"

He tried to scramble to his feet and, by leaning on the sled, managed to pull himself up.

"Perfectly all right," he muttered.

"You've been asleep. I've fed and watered both teams and they're ready to go. Here's hot tea. Your steak is about ready."

"I guess that disqualifies me," he said. They both knew he meant the rule that a musher must take sole care of his dogs had been broken when she fed his team.

"Don't be foolish. Aid can be given in an emergency on the trail. Was I supposed to let the huskies starve?"

Weylin swallowed the tea while Jenna went to get his steak. He'd failed. He, the man who always won.

"Damn it, Jenna," he called to her, "get back on the trail. If you don't care about coming in first, at least you can bring in those Maki Equipment dogs of mine you're driving."

Eleven

———

Jenna paid no attention to Weylin's urgings. Instead she followed his team back to Unalakleet and made certain he arrived safely at one of the homes open to mushers.

Okay, she told herself once she stepped onto the runners of her sled again, it's off to Nome.

She pulled out of Unalakleet only minutes ahead of Pete Hines. She'd been told that both Bucky and Charlie were ahead of her, Bucky by three hours. Could she catch them? Not Bucky, not unless he had trouble on the trail. Charlie? She could try.

She wasn't sorry, not for a second, about making love with Weylin, and for both of them she'd do her best to get her Maki team to Nome as quickly as she could. She had no chance, though, to come in first unless she stopped sleeping altogether and risked injury to the dogs by running them to their absolute limit.

Jenna shook her head. That wasn't fair to the animals, and she couldn't do it. Wouldn't do it. Winning wasn't that important, no matter what Weylin thought. Second would be a great accomplishment for anyone on her first Iditarod run; she'd try for that. Anyway, she'd really like to beat that chauvinist Charlie.

Of course Weylin wouldn't see second as an accomplishment. With him it was first or nothing. He might even scratch—drop from the race—in Unalakleet. No one would blame him; hypothermia was no joke. A shiver ran along her spine. What if she hadn't followed Chingo back to the salmon shack?

No, she warned herself. Keep your mind on the trail and on catching Charlie. Once you cross that finish line in Nome you can relax, but until then every thought, every motion has to be aimed at getting there.

Nome. A misnomer. The town was named after the cape to its east. The 1800s cartographer who mapped the Seward Peninsula had no idea what the cape was called and had scribbled, "Name?" next to it. Someone read the word wrong, and the map got published with "Cape Nome" printed on it.

I suppose that makes as much sense as calling the tallest mountain in the country McKinley because the man who did the naming liked President McKinley, she thought. She preferred the name Denali and wished those pushing for the change to the native name good luck.

Getting to Shaktoolik was an easy run. As Jenna started across frozen Norton Bay for Koyuk, slabs of fractured sea ice lay across one another and in the setting sun the ice was the translucent color of pale jade. To the west the Seward Peninsula reached toward Bering Strait; mountains rose to the east and north.

As she let Sonia choose the route, knowing the dog could sense the barely marked trail better than she, Jenna couldn't help remembering how Leonhard Seppala had crossed this bay with the diphtheria serum when the temperature was thirty degrees below zero. Even at ten above, the wind blowing across the ice chilled her to the bone.

She reached Koyuk near midnight. In the armory, where facilities were set up for the mushers, she found Charlie cooking for his dogs.

"Bucky's up the line, and we won't catch him," Charlie said, "so it looks like you or me for second. I hate to be the one to say it, but I ain't a gentleman."

"That's okay," she replied as she set up her stove. "On the trail I'm no lady either."

Despite Jenna's resolve not to sleep more than two hours, the warmth of the armory relaxed her and she crashed. If it hadn't been for Pete Hines's arrival waking her, she might have slept the clock around. As it was, she set out from Koyuk almost an hour behind Charlie.

"Only 150 miles to go," someone had printed on a cardboard sign near the outskirts of town.

Elim was the next stop. She made the forty-eight miles in seven hours and thought she should have done it in six. Her dogs weren't running as fast as they had earlier in the race. They were tired out, and so was she. Worse, Yetse, one of her wheelers, seemed to be favoring his left rear leg. And Favia, a swing dog and one of the speediest females in the team, was obviously limping.

Reluctantly, Jenna left Yetse and Favia in Elim to be cared for by the Iditarod crew, knowing the dogs would be shipped back to Anchorage by air as soon as possible.

She still had eleven dogs, six more than the minimum required when she arrived in Nome. Eleven dogs, though, can't pull a sled as fast as thirteen. And the trail to Golovin crossed the Bering Sea ice before making a tough portage through the Kwiktalik Mountains. Just before she reached Golovin in the teeth of an icy north wind, it began to snow.

Not daring to rest in Golovin because the storm might get worse while she slept and strand her there, she gave the dogs a snack and mushed on toward White Mountain, fighting snow and wind and an obliterated trail. And fighting her own fear that Sonia was as lost as she was and they'd never reach the checkpoint.

When the dogs slowed down, she was positive it was because Sonia had realized it was futile to go on. As the buildings of White Mountain loomed through the snow curtain, Jenna could hardly believe her eyes.

Charlie was sleeping when she entered the facility. She fed the dogs and ate herself, then hesitated. If she went on she'd be ahead of Charlie. But the dogs needed rest.

No, she thought, I'm not going to sacrifice the dogs. We'll stay over for at least two more hours.

Afraid to close her eyes for fear of oversleeping, Jenna pulled out of White Mountain light-headed with exhaustion but not far behind Charlie's twelve dogs. The snow had let up and Port Safety was ahead, the last checkpoint before Nome.

She reached Port Safety in the late afternoon of the fifteenth day of the race. There she chucked everything out of her sled that wasn't equipment required by the Iditarod committee and put on over her parka, the Number Two bib she'd gotten in Anchorage. The final twenty-two miles of trail were over sea ice again, around Cape Nome. As she pulled away from the town, Jenna saw Charlie no more than a few yards in front of Sonia. He was wearing his Number Twenty bib and was mushing eleven dogs—so he'd dropped one in Port Safety.

Darkness fell while Sonia was feeling her way along the ice. As she had many times during the long race, Jenna thought her life was literally in Sonia's paws. Sonia could follow an invisible trail in the dark and could sense the dangerous leads, the openings in the ice made by wind and ice pressure that could be wide enough for a sled to fall through.

After a while, Jenna lost all sense of where she was and had no idea whether Charlie was far ahead or just in front. Either way, she couldn't see him to pass him.

Nothing wrong with third, she assured herself. It could hardly make any difference to Weylin, since there was no way she could be first with Bucky so far in the lead. Bucky might even have crossed the finish line on Nome's Front Street by now.

When Sonia pulled off the ice and started uphill, Jenna, half dozing on the runners, was startled by the moan of a siren. She opened her eyes to bright lights and couldn't, for a moment or two, understand where she was.

Front Street! Nome!

"We made it!" she cried. "Sonia, all the rest of you fantastic guys, we made it!"

The lights were blinding after the darkness of the ice and Sonia faltered, looking around at Jenna. Jenna jumped off the runners and ran up and grabbed Sonia's neckline. "Come on, girl, the finish line's ahead. Don't pay any attention to all the fuss; I'm with you."

Running ahead of the dogs, she led them down the chute formed by snow fencing on both sides of the street. Crowds pressed against the fence pales, shouting and cheering. The finish line, an arch she had to pass under, was just ahead. She couldn't make out the words carved on it because of the glare of the lights, but she knew what they said.

"End of the Iditarod Dog Race, 1049 Miles, Anchorage to Nome."

A lump grew in Jenna's throat. Here she was. She'd driven her dogs across more than a thousand miles of wilderness. She'd run the Iditarod.

If only Weylin could have been with her. Or ahead of her.

As soon as she passed under the arch, she stopped the dogs, dropped to her knees, and threw her arms around Sonia's neck. Immediately all eleven huskies, tails wagging madly, did their best to jump on her and lick her face while the crowd laughed and cheered.

Untangling herself from the dogs and the lines, she walked to her sled and fumbled inside the cover. She pulled out the package of postmarked envelopes and brought it with her to hand to the mayor of Nome, symbolizing the delivery of the diphtheria serum so many years ago.

As officials came toward her, a man ran past them. She drew in her breath as she recognized him.

"Jenna!" Sam Matthews cried, opening his arms.

She flew into his embrace, tears running down her cheeks. "Oh, Sam," she sobbed, "I'm so glad to see you."

He patted her back.

"Ms Henderson," one of the officials said, and she was led away to a platform where microphones were thrust at her.

"How does it feel to be number two?"

"Is it true you're the first to place second in your maiden race?"

Jenna swallowed, wiping at her wet cheeks with a mittened hand and trying to regain her composure as she began to understand she'd actually come in second. She'd beaten Charlie after all.

"How did you do it?" an insistent newsman asked.

"Why, I stood on the runners and let the dogs pull me," she managed to say.

"Do you think Charlie Jones having to drop his lead dog in Safety helped you beat him?" he persisted.

His lead dog? Poor Charlie. "I don't think I could have gotten from Port Safety to Nome without *my* lead dog," she answered "Sonia brought me in second. I didn't have much to do with it."

The siren wailed again, signaling the approach of another musher. As the crowd's interest shifted to seeing whether it was Charlie, Jenna was able to leave the platform and get back to Sam. Sam ran interference for her, so she was able to plow through the crowd and into the warmth of race headquarters in the city hall.

"I left Weylin back in Unalakleet," she told Sam.

"I heard all about it. These dang reporters know everything, flying from one checkpoint to another like they do."

"Is he—is Weylin going to finish the race?"

"That's anyone's guess. Last I heard, he'd spent some time in bed but wasn't in any danger."

"He ought to fly back to Anchorage for medical care."

Sam shrugged. "Can't say what he'll do."

Jenna realized she hadn't even questioned Sam's presence in Nome.

"How did you come to be here?" she asked. "Does Weylin know you are?"

He shook his head. "I wanted to surprise you both. It's not every day my grandson and his girl compete in the longest dog sled race in the country. Besides, I always had this hankering to see Alaska. You know, it looks to be my kind of place."

"I'm glad you like Alaska." She wanted to tell him she wasn't Weylin's girl but wondered if maybe she was, now.

A painful longing to be with Weylin constricted her chest. Was he all right?

"I'd be proud to escort you to the banquet," Sam said. "They tell me Iditarod Week in Nome is one big party, and it sure seems to be true."

"I don't feel..."

"You have to go. Wouldn't do for a musher not to show up at her own party." Sam smiled at her. "Weylin always enjoyed a good party—you can pretend you're him."

He wouldn't enjoy it if he came in second, she thought. She was pleased and surprised to have beaten Charlie, but that wouldn't have been enough for Weylin.

"Weylin might have won," she said. "If he hadn't—" she paused. "Just what *did* you hear about him?"

"He got taken sick on the trail and had to go back to Unalakleet."

"Yes, that's what happened." Jenna was glad they'd missed the part she'd played, she couldn't have borne being questioned about it by the news media.

"You know that fellow who won this race—Bucky? He's quite a guy. Been running the Iditarod for five years now. He told them he enjoyed the trail, so why not? 'Like a vacation,' Bucky said, 'and if I come in the money I get paid for taking it.'"

"Some vacation." Would she do it again? Jenna wondered. She didn't think so; she'd proven to herself she could do it, proved herself as a dog trainer.

So why wasn't she more elated?

Because nothing could compare to what had happened between her and Weylin. Because he wasn't with her now.

"What are you going to do about Weylin?" she asked Sam.

"Stay here in Nome until I hear one way or the other."

"Then you think he'll try to finish?" Jenna shook her head. "He'd be so far behind. That wouldn't suit him at all. Anyway, he should fly out for medical care."

"I'll stay on," Sam repeated.

Jenna stayed on too. After a day and a half of practically uninterrupted sleep, she felt like a human being again and joined Sam at the festivities. She cheered on joggers running the cold, windswept beach in the Mukluk Minimarathon—five kilometers out and five back—for no more reward than the T-shirt that said they had run it, applauded the Frivolous Front Street Follies, a dancing and singing group at the Board of Trade Saloon; stood with the thinning crowds on Front Street to welcome in mushers who were now finishing past twentieth place and so were out of the money.

Finally every one of them was in Nome except Weylin.

She and Sam knew by then that he hadn't scratched and had left Unalakleet for Shaktoolik and gone on to Koyuk. Jenna pictured all sorts of disasters—Weylin dropping through a lead in the sea ice and drowning, Weylin overcome by exhaustion again and freezing to death.

When news came he was missing in a blizzard near White Mountain, she went to pieces, sobbing in despair on Sam's shoulder.

"He'll make it," Sam assured her. "He's a tough one."

"I've never even told him I love him," she cried. "Not so he understood. Oh, Sam, I can't bear it if anything's happened to him."

Two agonizing days later, a helicopter spotted Weylin on the trail to Port Safety. Ten days after Jenna had come in second, Weylin was due to arrive in Nome.

When, at the main banquet held three days previously, Jenna had watched the Golden Harness Award given to the best lead dog, she wanted to protest, to tell Chingo's story of finding her and leading her to Weylin. What other lead dog could match that?

But she said nothing. What had happened was private, between Weylin and her. Obviously he hadn't mentioned it, and neither would she. And Chingo didn't care one way or the other about a Golden Harness.

The media, noticeably reduced in numbers, appeared in the person of a TV newsman and a local reporter when it was announced that Weylin's team had been sighted on the ice, less than a mile away.

At noon, Jenna stood with Sam near the arch staring east along Front Street, straining for the first sight of Weylin's dogs.

At last she saw Chingo, and her heart leaped in joy. Weylin was safe, in a moment he'd be with her, everything was ending happily.

She bit back a gasp when the sled neared and she got her first look at his drawn, haggard face.

"Appears a mite peaked, I'd say," Sam muttered, "but that's some beard."

She nodded, unable to take her eyes from Weylin as he stepped off the runners to lead his dogs under the arch, officially finishing the Iditarod. The newsmen hurried toward him and, seeing them, she hung back. Sam stayed with her.

"Any comment on coming in last?" one asked.

"What're you going to do with your red lantern?" the other said.

Jenna had heard that the red lantern was the traditional prize for last place in a sled dog race, and she winced in sympathy with Weylin.

"I can't say last is as good as first," Weylin told them, "but I'm glad to get here."

Unable to contain herself any longer, Jenna pushed past the fence and ran to Weylin, flinging her arms around him and hugging him.

He held her away as he mustered up a tired smile. Then he looked over her shoulder and stiffened, letting her go. "Sam!" he exclaimed. "What in hell are you doing in Nome?"

Sam clasped Weylin in his arms, released him, and pounded him on the shoulder. "It's a great day for me, boy," he said. "I'm more proud of you at this moment than I ever have been before in my life."

Weylin stared at him. "But I'm last," he muttered finally.

"It's time you were last in something—do you a world of good." Sam's voice was gruff, and Jenna suspected he was fighting tears. "What I'm proud of is that you came in anyway, knowing you were last. Barely came in, by the looks of you. Come on, let's get you out of the cold."

Eating with them at the Bering Sea Saloon, Weylin glanced from Jenna to his grandfather. How could either of them be so damn happy?

Proud of him, Sam had said. The old man never lied, so Weylin had to believe him, but he didn't understand. Sam had only grunted in the past when, time after time, Weylin had won first-place trophies in diving, in tennis, in sailing. Sam had remained unimpressed when Weylin accumulated companies and made Whittaker Enterprises one of the wealthiest small corporations in the West. How could he possibly say he was proud to see Weylin come in last in a damn dog sled race in the backwoods of Alaska?

And Jenna. He could all but see the stars in her big brown eyes. She'd placed second; maybe it was because of that. It certainly couldn't be for his last-place finish.

"Great country," Sam said. "I'm thinking of getting myself a place in Alaska. I'm going to travel around the state some and make up my mind what part I like best."

"You don't need a place in Alaska," Weylin said.

"How do you know what I need? Julian's getting overrun with people from the city. If they keep building houses there, it'll wind up a San Diego suburb. I like peace and quiet. Lobo does too."

"You're exaggerating." Weylin heard the sharpness in his voice and sighed inwardly. He didn't mean to be brusque, but couldn't they see all he wanted was to be left alone?

He was tired. Sick and tired. Of dogs, of racing, of Alaska. What he needed was to be basking in the sun on a California beach all by himself.

They pitied him, that was it. Pity from Sam was bad enough, but he couldn't bear it from Jenna. Couldn't bear the look in those lovely eyes of hers.

Even though he was still hungry, he pushed away his plate. "I need some sleep," he said abruptly, rising. He strode away from the table, never once looking back.

Get away, get away. The phrase beat in his head like a drum. He left the restaurant, hailed a passerby, and asked where the airport was. He had to get away. Far away. And he had to get there now.

Twelve

———

Jenna stood in the Maki dog yard, her hand on Sonia's head. "You'll just have to come with me," she said. "I don't like to leave you here when I'm going to be gone for two days."

Sonia wriggled, pushing against Jenna's leg.

"I'll even let you ride in the front seat if you behave."

"Yow-owoo-oowoo," Sonia told her.

Jenna smiled. She unchained the dog and leashed her, then took her along to find Ron, the Maki dog caretaker.

If Weylin didn't like what she was doing, it was just too bad. He probably wouldn't even find out. Or care if he did. No one at Maki Equipment had seen him since before the Iditarod in early March, over two months before.

It had been almost two months since she'd seen him in Nome. Since then she hadn't had so much as a phone call or a letter from him. Sam had advised her to give Weylin time. Time for what? He'd obviously written off both her and Alaska.

Jenna caught sight of Ron filling water pans. "I'm taking Sonia with me. She'll be gone two days," she said.

Ron glanced from her to the husky and back. "You might get more than you bargained for," he advised.

"I can handle it. I'd just rather have her with me, one way or the other."

He shrugged. "It's all right with me. I'm not the boss."

As Jenna opened the passenger door of her car to let Sonia in, she wondered if she was doing the right thing—not by taking Sonia along but by going at all. Seeing Sam couldn't help but remind her of Weylin, and she was determined to shed no more tears over him.

Yet she liked and respected Sam, and she'd already turned down one invitation to visit him at his new cabin up near Palmer, thirty-eight miles northeast of Anchorage. She knew Sam was looking forward to seeing her, and it wasn't fair to punish him because of Weylin.

"You can mush on up here to my place," he'd told her on the phone the month before. "Plenty of room for the dogs."

Now it was May and there wasn't enough snow for a sled except in the mountains. For a time after returning from Nome she'd thought she might never want to stand on sled runners again, but she'd gotten over that. And gotten over her impulse to resign immediately from her position as Maki dog trainer.

The only thing she hadn't gotten over was Weylin Matthews.

Maybe she never would.

All the same, she had to live her life without him. The best way to begin was to start looking for another job. Her credentials as a trainer had been considerably enhanced by her second-place finish in the Iditarod, and she felt she ought to have no trouble. She'd really only stayed on this long at Maki because of Sonia.

Jenna headed out along Glenn Highway, remembering the winter day when she'd driven the dogs that way into Chugach State Park and had run into Weylin's team. They'd camped under the dancing northern lights and he'd shown her his new sleeping bag, big enough for two. She smiled a little, thinking how she'd fought against what they both wanted, how she'd slept primly alone in her own bag.

Her smile faded and tears pricked her eyes. In the hills near Norton Sound she hadn't slept alone. He'd held her, they'd made love; it had been the most beautiful night of her life. At the time she hadn't thought past her love for him; she'd believed it was a beginning. Instead, it had been an ending.

"Oh, Weylin," she whispered. "Why?"

Beside her, Sonia whined, her tongue lolling from her mouth.

Jenna took a deep breath, blinking back her tears. "You're too hot, aren't you? Wait, I'll roll down your window."

Cool May air blew into the car, a sign that the chill of winter had not been vanquished entirely, but the promise of spring underlay the coolness. Sonia put her muzzle out the window, looking backward.

Like I keep doing, Jenna admonished herself. I'm going to stop here and now. Weylin's the past. A dream. There's the present to get through and a future to look forward to.

A future without Weylin?

She clenched her teeth, focusing her attention on the highway. To her left the slaty water of Knik Arm glinted in the sun. To her right the Chugach peaks, still snow-capped, thrust into a picture-postcard blue sky where a pair of jets from Elmendorf Air Base trailed white vapor streamers.

Following Sam's directions, she drove into Palmer and turned off onto the old Glenn Highway.

"I'm only a couple of miles from town," he'd said, "but a hill or two gets in the way, and you wouldn't know there was another soul around."

His cabin should be easy to find. Peeled spruce logs, he'd told her, the ends dovetailed snugly, so new they hadn't yet weathered. "Young fellow built it for himself, then got married to a gal in Oregon who wasn't about to leave the Lower Forty-eight."

Sam had been there not quite a month and a half and already spoke like an Alaskan. She wondered how Weylin felt about his grandfather leaving Julian. Sam's no youngster, she thought with a flash of anger. The least Weylin could do was fly up and check on how he'd been getting along. But she knew Weylin hadn't.

She turned onto a gravel road, her car bouncing over frost heaves as she followed the drive into low hills. The cabin, she saw, was nestled between them. Several small birches, their white bark bright in the sun, had been planted in front of the house, with a sprinkling of dark green young spruce to either side.

As she pulled up in front, the cabin door opened and Sam came onto the porch, his white hair gleaming in the sun.

"I brought Sonia," she said. "I hope that's all right. I hated to leave her behind in Anchorage."

"Fine. No problem." He hurried down the steps toward her and gave her a bear hug. "You're looking great, Jenna."

Glancing down at her jeans and running shoes, she smiled ruefully. she'd worn an old red plaid jacket, a favorite of hers that Emily swore belonged in a rag-bag. Sam, she knew, hadn't expected her to dress up, since they planned to hike and maybe fish.

"You could be thirteen with your hair in pigtails like that," he added. "Do you want to bring Sonia in the house?"

Jenna shook her head. "She's not used to being inside. You said you had a couple of outbuildings—" she nodded to the right toward two sheds, one weathered gray, the second larger and newer "—and I thought I'd chain her outside one of them. If we leave the shed door open she can go inside if she wants to."

He nodded. "Might as well get her comfortable before you come in. I know you won't relax until you do."

Sonia accepted being tethered to the smaller shed without protest and when Sam opened the door, she stuck her head inside, sniffing warily.

"We'll let her investigate," he said. "Nothing in there she can harm or that'll hurt her. You can fix her a bed later."

Inside the cabin, Jenna exclaimed over the golden oak furniture. "Where did you find such gorgeous antiques?"

"These are replicas of oak furniture my folks used to own," Sam said. "I found a place in Seattle that made them. Got to be careful these days. You can't tell the real thing from a replica."

Jenna turned away from him on the pretense of admiring an oak mantel clock, afraid Sam would see her distress. As far as she'd been concerned, what she had with Weylin had been real. Yet it seemed she must have been mistaken. For a moment her heart hurt so she put a hand to her chest.

She heard a whine, heard Sam open a door, and the next she knew Lobo was at her side, studying her with his slanted yellow eyes. She held her hand to him and he sniffed it, then permitted her to touch his head.

For an instant Jenna could almost see Weylin crouched on the floor as he had in Julian, with his arms around Lobo's neck and the wolf nuzzling him. Tears sprang to her eyes.

"He remembers you, all right," Sam said.

Lobo might remember, but Weylin had forgotten her. She swallowed a sob. A hand touched her shoulder and she turned to Sam, trying to muster a smile.

He shook his head. "You don't have to put on for me. Thought the boy'd get over it by now. The thing is—he's ashamed to face you."

"Did he tell you that?"

"No. Stands to reason though. You beat him, and it was your first time in the Iditarod too. He challenged Alaska and he lost. Weylin's not used to losing. He'll shape up, given time."

No, she thought. Sam didn't know all that had gone on, didn't know about her rescue of Weylin and what had happened between them afterward. Their lovemaking had nothing to do with winning or losing. At least she hadn't believed it did at the time, but she'd been wrong about everything else.

"Now that I get a good look at you," Sam said, "I see you're a mite peaked. I've got just the remedy for that. Some of Estelle's blueberry pie and a cup of my coffee. I may not make the best coffee in the world, but I make the strongest."

"Estelle?" Jenna asked, doing her best to respond to Sam's change of subject.

"Estelle Swenson. She lives a mile or so up the road, all by herself. We got acquainted when she saw me hiking with Lobo. Makes a first-rate pie." Sam cleared his throat and shifted his feet. "Fact is, I've asked her to supper."

Oh-ho, Jenna said to herself. "I'll enjoy meeting Estelle," she told him. "I meant to ask you—did you have any problem getting Lobo to Alaska? I wondered if they'd let you transport a wolf without a lot of red tape."

"I didn't call him a wolf; said he was my dog. No use going out of your way to look for trouble. He's not that much different than half the dogs I see up here anyway, except he doesn't have a curled-up tail. Come on, let's taste the pie."

Jenna did her best with the delicious pie and, later, with the evening meal. Estelle turned out to be a gray-haired, no-nonsense widow in her sixties. Her alert blue eyes noted how little Jenna ate, but neither she nor Sam mentioned it. Jenna suspected Sam might have discussed her with Estelle. It was obvious the two took to each other.

She was happy for Sam, she told herself, yet watching the way they smiled at each other made her feel worse than ever.

"I think I'll check on Sonia again," Jenna said after Estelle chased her out of the kitchen, insisting she was going to wash the dishes and have Sam wipe them.

Sonia had been asleep, curled nose to tail, but yawned and stretched when Jenna approached. "Okay, I'll let you rest," she said, after petting the husky for a few minutes.

They'd eaten late, but since it was May, the evenings had begun to stretch into the night. In Anchorage the sun would be setting over the Sleeping Lady, Mount Susitna. Here it was hidden by the Talkeetna Mountains but tinted the clouds salmon pink.

Jenna left Sonia and walked up the hill behind Sam's cabin, shoving her gloved hands in her jacket pockets against the cool breeze. The wind at the top was downright cold, and Jenna hurried down the lee side to where a few cottonwoods huddled together, their new green leaves fluttering as the branches swayed.

Spring. A beginning, a starting over. She had to exorcise her love for Weylin before she could begin anew. Jenna hit her fist against a trunk. How? It was like being buried under an avalanche. No matter how she struggled to release from his spell, she couldn't fight free.

She closed her eyes, picturing Weylin as she'd first seen him, in his wolf-trimmed parka, gliding on snowshoes out of the darkness into the light of her campfire, his green eyes glinting.

He'd captured her then, only she hadn't realized what had happened to her until much later. She was like the woman with the pentagram on her palm, the woman whose fate it was to fall victim to the were-wolf. She'd been Weylin's victim, exactly as he'd told her in Julian.

She still was.

A dog began to bark, and her eyes snapped open. Sonia? Yes, but it was a warning bark; likely a rabbit had ventured close to the shed.

Jenna, starting to relax, tensed again when a long, quavering howl rose into the evening air. That wasn't Sonia; that was a wolf.

Well, of course it was. It was Lobo. Wasn't it?

The howling came again, a lonesome, eerie cry that, once heard, is never forgotten.

Sonia's half-howl, half-bark joined Lobo's.

Jenna's view of the cabin was cut off by the hill. Should she return? If nothing was wrong, she hated to rejoin Sam and Estelle just yet. It was too painful to see the warmness between them, even though she was delighted for Sam's sake.

The clamor died away and Jenna hesitated, finally leaning against the cottonwood trunk again. Whatever had disturbed the animals was gone.

She gazed out over the Matanuska Valley, seeing King Mountain's snow-capped peak rosy in the setting sunlight. Sam, as old as he was, had responded to the beauty of Alaska. Why couldn't Weylin? Was it true, as Sam had said, that Weylin felt defeated by Alaska? She had difficulty believing anything would make Weylin feel defeated. At least not for long.

Oh, God, was she to go through her entire life unable to keep Weylin out of her thoughts for more than two minutes at a time?

She glanced back toward the top of the hill. A dark figure stood silhouetted against the evening sky. It could only be Sam, worried about her and come to look for her.

"I'm here," she called, waving.

He came toward her, and she admonished herself for letting Sam see how distraught she'd been earlier. It had upset him enough to make him feel he had to check on her.

But wasn't he too tall to be Sam?

A wolf cry broke the silence, startling her with its closeness. If she hadn't known better, she'd swear the howling came from the approaching man.

She knew only one man who could howl like that.

"No," she whispered. "No, it can't be."

Down the hill he came, closer and closer, lean and lithe and dangerous. Her breath caught in her throat, her heart hammered in her ears. She couldn't move, couldn't speak. Struck dumb because the wolf had seen her first...

As he neared her tree he slowed, then stopped less than a foot away. "You've put me to a lot of trouble, Jenna Henderson," Weylin growled.

She gathered herself together. "Has it ever occurred to you that the feeling might be mutual?" To her amazement the words emerged crisp and clear.

"I refuse to believe you've been as miserable as I have. How was I expected to understand what had hold of me? Love's a madness with so many disguises a man can't recognize it right off. Desire, I told myself. Good, healthy lust. Well, it was that too. That and more. So damn much more I panicked."

He took another step toward her, bringing him so close she could see the glow in his green eyes, as though they were lit from within.

"You lost first place in the Iditarod to save me," he said, his voice harsh, "and you didn't mind. Later, when I was on the final run to Nome, I asked myself, if I'd been running first, what I would have done if you needed me somewhere back along the trail. The answer was that I'd have gone back—how could I bear to lose you? But would I have gone back without resentment? I couldn't answer that one.

"So there you were in Nome, you and Sam, both of you so damn glad to see me. Sam was saying he was proud of me and you were welcoming me with those velvety eyes of yours, neither of you caring I was dead last. It was like drowning and having your entire life flash before you. What kind of life had I lived? What was important? Jenna, I got scared as hell and I ran."

"Apparently you've recovered." Was this really her voice? The flat, dry tone seemed to be a stranger's.

He shook his head. "I'm never going to recover." He reached for her hand, turning it palm up. "The only future I have is written there." He moved closer, his eyes holding hers. "You told me on the trail that there were things in life more important than winning, and I didn't agree. Winning was my life." He took a deep breath. "No longer." He smiled wryly. "Not that I'll make a good loser."

His fingers touched her cheek. Jenna trembled with the effort not to react as his potent allure electrified her, taking her breath away, heating her blood, surrounding her with the enchantment only Weylin could bring to her.

"You're my life, Jenna," he murmured. "Without you, there's nothing. You're more important than anything I have or ever will have. Is it too late to tell you?"

His lips were only inches away from hers, and she had to clear her throat before she could speak. Even then her words were husky. "Don't you smell my wolfsbane perfume? Who else would I wear it for?"

She saw the white slash of his grin and had an instant to realize he'd shaved off the beard but left a mustache before she was crushed in his arms, his mouth on hers asking, taking, giving. She surrendered herself to the wonder of his embrace. Desire budded, flowered, a wild, rampant growth nourished by the magic of his body pressed to hers.

A long-drawn-out yipping howl of fright and pain galvanized her. She broke away. "Sonia!" She gasped. "She needs us. Come on!" Jenna grabbed his hand and began running up the hill.

Minutes later they were at the shed. Sonia was inside, growling.

"Shh, it's all right, Sonia, it's Jenna. Jenna and Weylin. You know us. We won't hurt you, we're here to help." Keeping her voice low and soothing, Jenna went on talking, flicking on the lantern she'd left near the door, and edged inside.

Sonia was crouched on an old blanket over the straw bed Jenna had fixed for her, still growling a little deep in her throat. Not at Jenna though; the snarl seemed directed at the discomfort Sonia was having as the head and then the body of a black puppy pushed from her onto the blanket.

"My God, she's having pups," Weylin said from behind Jenna. He paused a minute. "I think I remember being told a dog's gestation period's about sixty days. That means—" He stopped and began to laugh. "The same night?" he asked.

"I think so. She and Chingo were harnessed next to each other for hours."

"I'll be damned."

They watched in silence. Weylin held Jenna around the waist as she stood with her back to him, while the husky delivered another black pup, then three fawn-and-white puppies, licking each clean with her tongue as soon as it was born and severing the cord with her teeth.

"This is her first litter," Jenna said, "and she's doing a marvelous job. She'll be a good mother."

"Instinct," Weylin murmured into her ear, sliding his hands underneath her jacket. "How's yours?"

"Mine?" She turned to face him, puzzled.

"Think you'd make a good mother? We can't let Sonia and Chingo outdo us like this."

"I wouldn't care to have more than one at a time. And before I think about that, aren't there a few things we haven't settled?"

"We can get married as soon as the state of Alaska allows. One day? Three?" He nuzzled her neck, taking tiny nips.

"But you hate Alaska," she wailed.

"I'm coming to have a grudging respect for this country. We'll bargain. So much time in California for so much time in Alaska. Deal?"

"That sounds fair, but..."

"And, if you'll remember to lock me up when the moon is full, I can promise babies, not cubs. Deal?"

Jenna flung her arms around his neck, laughing. "Deal," she agreed.

WHAT LIES BEYOND PARADISE?

tching the pulse of a
man in the Twenties.
A woman with a dream.
man with all his dreams
ttered. The search for a
g-lost father. And the
covery of love.
Available from 14th
rch 1986. Price £2.50.

ORLDWIDE

Silhouette Desire

COMING NEXT MONTH

TANGLED WEB
Lass Small

How could Peggy possibly let herself fall for a man who thought she was another woman? On the other hand, when Joe was the man, how could she possibly not?

HAWK'S FLIGHT
Annette Broadrick

The man who had nursed her during her concussion claimed to be both her pilot and her new husband. Paige couldn't remember getting married, but lying in Hawk Cameron's gentle, passionate embrace felt so right.

TAKEN BY STORM
Laurien Blair

When Nick Jarros thundered into Randy Wade's office she wished she could hide underneath the desk. It was either that or throw herself into his arms. Not only was her professional reputation at stake — so was her heart!

Silhouette Desire

COMING NEXT MONTH

LOOK BEYOND TOMORROW
Sara Chance

Isis O'Shea usually had a sixth sense about
people, but from the moment the rather
conservative James Leland first appeared in her
Lake Tahoe audience, he was an enigma.

A COLDHEARTED MAN
Lucy Gordon

It had been ten years, but one look in Valerio's dark
eyes and it seemed like yesterday. Time had not
softened the pain, nor had it diminished the passion.
Now the one man who had just cause to hate Helena
held her fate in his hands.

NAUGHTY, BUT NICE
Jo Ann Algermissen

Born on opposite sides of the tracks, Tamara and
Damon had moved in the same direction — carrying
a secret yearning. No two people could be more
different.....But there are no rules in the lesson of
love.

Silhouette Desire

MARCH TITLES

GOLDEN GODDESS
Stephanie James

RIVER OF DREAMS
Naomi Horton

TO HAVE IT ALL
Robin Elliot

LEADER OF THE PACK
Diana Stuart

FALSE IMPRESSIONS
Ariel Berk

WINTER MEETING
Doreen Owens Malek

Silhouette Desire Romances

TAKE 4
THRILLING SILHOUETTE
DESIRE ROMANCES
ABSOLUTELY FREE

Experience all the excitement, passion and pure joy of love. Discover fascinating stories brought to you by Silhouette's top selling authors. At last an opportunity for you to become a regular reader of Silhouette Desire. You can enjoy 6 superb new titles every month from Silhouette Reader Service, with a whole range of special benefits, a free monthly Newsletter packed with recipes, competitions and exclusive book offers. Plus information on the top Silhouette authors, a monthly guide to the stars and extra bargain offers.

**An Introductory FREE GIFT for YOU.
Turn over the page for details.**

As a special introduction we will send you FOUR
specially selected Silhouette Desire romances
— yours to keep FREE — when you complete
and return this coupon to us.

At the same time, because we believe that you will be so thrilled
with these novels, we will reserve a subscription to Silhouette
Reader Service for you. Every month you will receive 6 of the very
latest novels by leading romantic fiction authors, delivered direct to
your door.

Postage and packing is always completely
free. There is no obligation or commitment —
you can cancel your subscription at any time.

It's so easy. Send no money now. Simply fill in and post
the coupon today to:-

**SILHOUETTE READER SERVICE, FREEPOST,
P.O. Box 236 Croydon, SURREY CR9 9EL**

Please note: READERS IN SOUTH AFRICA to write to:-
Silhouette, Postbag X3010 Randburg 2125 S. Africa

- -

FREE BOOKS CERTIFICATE

To: Silhouette Reader Service, FREEPOST, PO Box 236,
Croydon, Surrey CR9 9EL

Please send me, Free and without obligation, four specially selected Silhouette Desire Romances and reserve a
Reader Service Subscription for me. If I decide to subscribe, I shall, from the beginning of the month following my
free parcel of books, receive six books each month for £5.94, post and packing free. If I decide not to subscribe I
shall write to you within 10 days. The free books are mine to keep in any case. I understand that I may cancel my
subscription at any time simply by writing to you. I am over 18 years of age.
Please write in BLOCK CAPITALS.

Name _____

Address _____

_____

_____ Postcode _____

SEND NO MONEY — TAKE NO RISKS
*Remember postcodes speed delivery. Offer applies in U.K. only
and is not valid to present subscribers. Silhouette reserve the right
to exercise discretion in granting membership. If price changes
are necessary you will be notified.
Offer limited to one per household. Offer expires April 30th, 1986.*

EP18SD